May

For Chris—

With every good wish to a fine (albeit not feathered) friend!

All the best,

Ray

The Audubon Quartet

Other books by Ray Sipherd

Dance of the Scarecrows

The Christmas Store

The Courtship of Peggy McCoy

The Audubon Quartet

Ray Sipherd

St. Martin's Press
New York

A THOMAS DUNNE BOOK.
An imprint of St. Martin's Press.

 For information, address St. Martin's Press, 175 Fifth Avenue, New York, N.Y. 10010.

Library of Congress Cataloging-in-Publication Data

Sipherd, Ray.
The Audubon quartet / by Ray Sipherd. — 1st ed.
p. cm.
"A Thomas Dunne book"—T.p. verso.
ISBN 0-312-18536-7
I. Title.
PS3569.I59A94 1998
813'.54—dc21 97-53087
CIP

First Edition: May 1998

10 9 8 7 6 5 4 3 2 1

For

Eleanor Ruth Kelly

Acknowledgments

WITH SPECIAL THANKS to Milan G. Bull, Director, Connecticut Audubon Society, Fairfield, Connecticut; Michael V. Carlisle, The William Morris Agency; Neal Bascomb and Tom Dunne, St. Martin's Press; Drs. Steven Herbert, B. Joseph Meehan, and Turpin H. Rose; Ms. Craigin Bowen, Deputy Director, The Straus Center for Conservation and Technical Studies, Cambridge, Massachusetts; Ms. Margaret Tamulonis, The New York Historical Society; Ms. Kathryn Wiebusch, The Metropolitan Museum of Art, New York; Messrs. Seth O.L. Brody and Seth L. Cooper—and, as always, Anne Marie.

Rogues though they be, and thieves . . . see how each is enjoying the fruits of his knavery . . .

JOHN JAMES AUDUBON
Ornithological Biography,
Volume II, 1832

The Audubon Quartet

Prologue

THE FOG.

Moments earlier, the horizon had spread outward to infinity, the line as sharp and certain as a razor stroke. As the ship had glided from Hyannis Harbor in mid-afternoon, the weather had been warm, the sky the creamy blue of a robin's egg. Everywhere Jon looked there had been boats—sailboats and pleasure cruisers, runabouts and trawlers; even an intrepid windsurfer, who had ventured far from shore to take advantage of the first full summer weekend of the year.

All that was about to change. Soon, sea and sky would be rewoven seamlessly into a vast cloak of thick, impenetrable gray.

Jon Wilder stood alone at the bow of the *Eagle,* the largest of the ferries that connected Cape Cod to the island of Nantucket, thirty miles to the south, and watched as the ship approached the fog.

He had first come to Nantucket as a child to visit his maternal grandmother, who lived in Siasconset, on the island's eastern edge. In the intervening years, he had grown taller, well over six feet; his dark hair had become grayer, the lines around his eyes and jaw more deeply etched. On this visit he would not build castles in the sand or splash along the surf at Codfish Park as he had once done.

Still, as the ship sped on, he felt a special fondness for the island that those memories evoked. The *Eagle* had been sailing for two hours. At this point in the voyage, the long profile of Nantucket's northern coastline should be visible—the houses along Cliffside, the water tower at Dionis, the moors that undulated west to Eel Point. Instead, all had been devoured by the fog.

The ship slowed. The foghorn began sounding out its mournful call.

Looking down over the rail, Jon saw that the water had a gray, dull, leaden flatness, broken only by the rippling white wake extending outward from the ferry's prow.

Then suddenly the fog seized them like a fist. Jon felt its wet, cold fingers squeezing, tightening around them, carrying the ship and everyone aboard toward what, he did not know.

He remembered what his grandmother had called the sea fog that swept over the island, particularly in the spring and summer months: "Nantucket porridge" was the quaint phrase she had used. So thick, she'd told him, you could stir it with a spoon. As a child, he had thought of it as warm and comforting, in the way porridge ought to be.

But this fog chilled him. It aroused a fear in him as real and as tangible as any he had ever known.

The ship slowed further, altering her course. Were they entering the harbor? No, it was too soon.

Or, was there something out there, something they now

sought to avoid? Was it another ship? An object the ferry's radar had detected, one no human eye could see?

Or was it something else entirely? Something beckoning them. Something they would be unable to escape, no matter what their course.

1

THE FERRY SLIPPED between the pilings of her berth; the engines whirred, then ceased. Chains rattled.

In the enclosed cabin above the main deck where vehicles were parked, the passengers rose and collected their belongings. Some headed to their cars. Others formed into a makeshift line, waiting for the gangway and the stairs at dockside that would bring them to the broad macadam wharf.

Lorelei Merriwell moved out into the aisle. "I'm going to freshen up before they let us off the boat," she said to Jon.

"Sure. Go ahead. It'll be several minutes anyway." He added, "Maybe I'll go out on deck and see what I can make out of the town in all this fog."

She turned, brushed back her long blond hair, and headed off. Jon watched her go: the slim and graceful woman who had come into his life a few years earlier and was today so much a part of it he found it difficult to remember the time he'd spent without her friendship and her company.

He crossed to the port side of the ferry, opened the heavy steel door and stepped onto the deck. In spite of the fog—or because of it—the scene evoked more recollections from the past: the gray, wood-shingled buildings, and the narrow cobblestone streets, whose paving blocks had served as ballast for the ships that had made this harbor home more than a century ago.

"Excuse me," Jon heard someone say.

He turned to see a man approach the rail. Appearing to be in his seventies, the man was reasonably stout and wore a navy double-breasted blazer with some sort of insignia on the breast pocket. The yachting cap above a thatch of white hair bore the same design. In his hand he gripped the silver handle of a walking stick. As the man edged against the rail, Jon saw that his face was ruddy and had a small mustache that curved upward at the ends.

"Mind if I join you?" the man asked.

"Not at all," Jon said.

"I always love this vista of the harbor from the boat," the man continued. "I've lived here for more years than I can count and never tire of the scene. My wife calls me the island's biggest booster. But I'm a friendly man by nature, I'll admit." He turned to Jon. "But I assume you're an off-islander?"

"Yes. I'm from Connecticut."

"No need to apologize," the man assured him. "Welcome to Nantucket nonetheless. We've become more hospitable the last few hundred years. I'm told before that, the natives slaughtered whole boatloads of people from the mainland. Nantucket is an Indian word meaning 'the faraway land.' Did you know that?"

He thrust a beefy hand in Jon's direction. "My name is Swain. Thomas Swain. Or Commodore Swain, if you like titles. I received it after I helped found the Cliffside Yacht Club. The rank is purely honorary, but it looks impressive on a letterhead. And you are?"

"Jon Wilder."

"You're not related to the Wilders in brokerage, by any chance?"

"No."

"Or is it banking?" The man pondered. "In any case, Nantucket draws the quiet money. Always has. Not like her sister to the west."

He gave a vague, dismissive wave toward Martha's Vineyard. "Those people on the other island will let anybody in. Nantucket is far more discerning. My family's had a house along the bluff for years. Is this your first trip?"

"No. I was here as a boy," Jon said.

"So what brings you this time?"

"A friend is hosting an art gallery reception on Wide Wharf this afternoon. We're taking the late ferry back."

"Too bad," Swain said. "To come all this way, I mean, and then have to return. Next time you must stay longer."

"I'd like to."

"Do you sail, by the way?" Swain asked.

"I haven't recently. But I enjoy it."

"Then you should make it a priority when you come back. These waters are wonderful for sailing, and the island boasts some of the best sailors in the world. Think of Starbuck, the first mate on the whaling ship in *Moby Dick.* He was a Nantucketer."

The commodore's face glowed with pride. "In fact, when you're next visiting, go to the office of my yacht club and mention me. They'll find you something suitable."

"Thanks. I'll keep it in mind."

The man bent closer to Jon, squinting. "Wilder. Jonathan McNicol Wilder. You're not that fellow who paints birds?"

"Yes."

"I should have known. I saw the picture of you in your *Guide to Eastern Birds.* Of course, you're older than your photo indicates. Still, my wife will be delighted that we met. She's a birder herself and a great fan of yours."

"I'm pleased to hear that."

"In fact, when you're on Nantucket again, do stop by and have a drink with us."

He fished through an inside pocket of his blazer, withdrew a leather card case and plucked out a card. "Here's our address and telephone. Call anytime."

Jon took the card and thanked him.

"And remember what I said about the sailing," Swain reminded him.

"I will."

"Splendid." The commodore touched the brim of his cap, turned and marched in the direction of the door, the walking stick producing rhythmic taps along the deck.

DISEMBARKING FROM THE ferry, Jon and Lorelei headed quickly in the direction of Wide Wharf. As they crossed Easy Street, the fog seemed even thicker, glistening the cobblestones and curling in the doorways of the old buildings near the pier.

"So tell me more about the man who's giving this reception," Lorelei said as they walked.

"His name is Brian Ravener," Jon told her. "He's a very special friend. He saved my life."

"That qualifies. What happened?"

"Some years ago I was painting birds along the outer beaches of Cape Cod. It was a hot day in July, so I decided to go in for a swim. Suddenly my legs cramped; I tried rubbing them, but I was being carried out to sea. Brian happened to be walking on the beach, saw me, and swam out and rescued me. Later, he invited me to visit him in Boston and we've been friends ever since."

"He sounds like quite a man."

"He is," Jon said admiringly. "He's also a self-made millionaire. As a young man, he invented some sort of electronic gadget for computers, patented it, and the money started to roll in. He could retire, but he has too much energy to sit around."

"You said he lives in Boston?"

"Beacon Hill. He also has a house here on the far side of the harbor."

"And he's an art collector, obviously."

"He began collecting maybe a dozen years ago," Jon said. "He has no formal training, but his eye for quality is excellent."

They turned onto New Whale Street and walked in the direction of Wide Wharf.

The wharf, as its name indicated, was the broadest and busiest of the half-dozen others that jutted out into the harbor. In the nineteenth century, when whaling was the island's principal and most profitable industry, it had been the anchorage of whalers and commercial sailing ships. Today it was as active, but in a very different way. Now shops, restaurants, and boutiques bordered the brick walkway that served as a promenade. As Lorelei and Jon continued along it, he read the signs: Nantucket Nauticals, a ship's chandlery; The Old Kite Shoppe; a harborside coffeehouse that called itself The Sea Cup; and Barnacle

Bill's Fish and Chowder, advertising the best steamers on the island. The gallery was at the end of the wharf, in a single-story building of gray wooden shingles and white trim.

As they approached it, a horn sounded behind them, urging everyone to move aside. As they did, a white limousine slid past and stopped outside the gallery.

"I didn't think cars were allowed on Wide Wharf," Lorelei observed.

"They're not," Jon said.

The chauffeur leaped out of the limousine and opened a rear door. At the same moment, a man in a tuxedo emerged from the door opposite. He was in his sixties, quite tall and extremely tan. But his most distinguishable feature was his absolutely hairless head; not only was he completely bald, but there was no hint whatsoever of eyelashes or eyebrows, giving him a slightly androidal appearance.

From the door the chauffeur had opened, a woman in a long evening dress stepped out. She was at least twenty years younger than the man, auburn-haired and elegantly beautiful in a remote, patrician sort of way. She took the arm of the tuxedoed man, who had now joined her.

Lorelei regarded them with curiosity and fascination. "I know who the man is. Daddy Warbucks."

"Daddy Warbucks ought to be so rich," Jon said. "That's Myles Coleridge. He's one of the leading art collectors in the country. He owns several of my paintings of birds. We've also met from time to time at gallery receptions and arts benefits."

"I can see the woman isn't Little Orphan Annie."

"It's his wife, Meredith." He added, "She was married years ago to Brian Ravener."

Lorelei gave Jon a wry glance. "That should make for an interesting evening."

The Coleridges walked toward the gallery, her arm in his. As they entered, there were bursts of light from inside—flash photos being taken of the pair. More people followed in their wake.

Moving through the door themselves, Jon and Lorelei were stopped immediately by the crush of people inside. Looking around, Jon saw that the attire of the guests ranged from formal wear to lacy minis for the younger women, as well as T-shirts, Speedo pants and sandals for the men. In his white linen suit, Jon felt uniquely overdressed.

The gallery appeared to be divided into two large rooms. Against a side wall of the room in which they stood, there was a bar. Reception guests surrounded it four deep. Trays of hors d'oeuvres, held aloft by serving people, wafted as if airborne just above the crowd.

"Jon!" a voice boomed. From behind, Jon felt his shoulders being seized.

He turned and discovered himself face-to-face with Brian Ravener. Dressed in an elegant tuxedo with a ruffled shirt and broad bow tie, the man was a commanding presence—the huge frame and powerful, broad chest; the full head of black hair touched with gray; and beneath it, the intense blue eyes.

He took Jon's hand and pumped it vigorously. "Jon, my friend—I'm glad you're here."

"How are you, Brian?" Jon turned to Lorelei. "I'd like you to meet Lorelei Merriwell."

"Very pleased indeed." Ravener bowed graciously. "You're as beautiful as Jon described you. I amend that. *More* so."

Lorelei smiled. "Thank you."

Looking beyond Ravener, Jon saw a slim, attractive woman in a green sheath dress approaching them. Her dark hair was knotted in a tight chignon. Standing slightly behind Ravener, she put her fingers lightly on his arm.

"Brian, honey—here you are!" Her voice had a mellow Southern lilt.

Ravener turned and put his arm around the woman's waist. "Jon, Lorelei—this is the lovely lady who has made this evening possible. I'd like you to meet Ariel McKenzie, owner of the Wide Wharf Gallery." He repeated the introductions all around.

Finally, the woman looked at Ravener again. "Brian, do remember what you promised me."

"Would you excuse me?" Ravener said. "Ariel wants me to keep hobnobbing with her artsy-fartsy friends."

"Brian, shame on you . . ." Ariel McKenzie gave a little laugh.

"The front room of the gallery contains the current show," Ravener concluded before leaving. "Pieces from my collection of bird art are in the second room, along with a few recent acquisitions. Get some champagne or whatever at the bar. Then come on back."

A sly smile crossed his face. "I have some announcements to make." He took Ariel McKenzie's hand and headed off.

A short time later, each carrying tall flutes of champagne, Lorelei and Jon continued on into the second room. It was even more crowded than the first. If works from Ravener's collection were on display, it was virtually impossible to see them, given the number of people in the room.

Then the group nearest to them parted and Jon saw Myles Coleridge and his wife approaching. Under the bright ceiling lights, Coleridge's head had the appearance of a Spauldeen ball.

"Good evening, Jon," he announced, smiling. "Anything of yours here?"

"Several pieces, I was told. We haven't had a chance to look." Jon nodded to Lorelei. "Myles, this is Mrs. Merriwell."

Coleridge gave a courtly nod. "Delighted, Mrs. Merriwell." He gestured to his wife. "Both of you, I'd like you to meet my wife, Meredith."

He was about to go on with the introductions when they were confronted by a wiry young man in a safari jacket, who without warning pushed a camera in their faces.

"Come on, folks!" the photographer urged. "Party time—let's smile!" There was a burst of light, followed by two more.

Jon was immediately blinded. When his eyes finally readjusted, the young man was gone, as were Coleridge and his wife. Instead, he made out the figure of a dough-faced woman in a flowered caftan standing next to him.

"My apologies," the woman said. "Pesky Swift happens to be my best photographer, but he's unsubtle when it comes to candid shots."

She turned to face Jon. "I'm Diana Cardigan. You may remember that our magazine did a piece about you several years ago."

"Yes," Jon said. "Diana—this is Mrs. Merriwell. Lorelei—Diana Cardigan. Ms. Cardigan is the feature editor of *Au Courant.*"

"Are you also an artist?" the woman asked Lorelei.

"No," Lorelei said. "I have an antiques shop in Scarborough, Connecticut."

"The town where Jon lives," Diana Cardigan remarked. "I suppose the two of you are lovers." Seeing Lorelei's surprised embarrassment, she patted Lorelei's arm. "Don't worry, my dear. I won't put that in the photo caption."

"Is *Au Courant* covering tonight's event?" Jon asked.

The woman nodded. "We do a lot of art receptions and they're all the same. Given the inflated egos of the guests, it's like being a spectator at a hot-air balloon rally. Tonight's attendees are your typical art glitterati—BPAWs—the Beautiful People of the Art World."

She scanned the crowd. ". . . And one person," she continued, "who is very ugly."

Jon looked in the direction that Diana Cardigan had fixed her gaze. Against a side wall, standing alone, was a short man in a polyester jacket and ill-matching slacks, examining a painting of a shrike. The man's round face was rough-skinned, resembling a melon to which facial features had been stuck. The lips were sensual but weak, the eyes protuberant.

"See him?" she asked Lorelei and Jon. "The one who looks like Peter Lorre with a bad makeover."

"Who is he?" Lorelei said.

"Abel Lasher is his name. You know him, don't you, Jon?" she asked.

Jon shook his head. "Not really. I know who he is, but I've never had anything to do with him."

"Consider yourself blessed." Diana Cardigan turned back to Lorelei. "Jon will give you a kinder description of the man than I will. But Abel Lasher is one of the most hated men in the art world. He failed as an artist, as the owner of a gallery, and as an agent trying to sell other people's art. When he realized his own name was a pun, he decided to become a critic. Lash he did, but able he was not. Four years ago, he founded his own magazine, *Art Now,* so he could spew his venom through the printed word."

She leaned closer. "Keep out of his way, Jon," she advised. "Particularly if you hear the rattle in his tail starting to twitch."

Diana Cardigan moved off, her caftan flowing as she went.

Her place was occupied by a thin man in his fifties with gray hair, a neatly trimmed gray beard, and dark glasses of the wrap-around kind.

"Jon Wilder—" the man began, giving Jon's name a distinctly British sound. "We met at a one-man show of mine in Providence last fall. Jack Briscoe."

"Yes," Jon answered noncommittally.

The man was a true symphony in affectation—off-white silk shirt unbuttoned well down, which allowed the gold chains and ankh pendant to be seen, stone-washed designer jeans, a leather-tooled belt, and espadrilles.

Briscoe smiled now at Lorelei. "And this is?"

"Mrs. Merriwell," she volunteered.

His hand came forward, grasping hers. But instead of shaking it, he brought it to his lips and kissed it. "Charmed," he purred. "Are you by any chance an artists' model, Mrs. Merriwell?"

"No," Lorelei said, taking back her hand.

"You could be," Briscoe told her. "Be that as it may, if you're both staying for the weekend, do come out to my beach house in Quaise. I can show you some of the new things I'm working on."

"We're taking the late ferry back tonight," Jon said.

"Another time, then." Briscoe answered airily. At that moment, a beautiful young woman came into the room. His eyes responded like a raptor spotting prey.

"Excuse me," he told Jon and Lorelei, and eased off in the direction of the girl.

The next instant, a shrill whistle pierced the air. At the far end of the room, Brian Ravener appeared above the crowd. He put his fingers to his lips, produced another whistle, then a third, until the room was absolutely still.

From where Jon stood, he guessed that Ravener was on some sort of platform. Also, for the first time, he noticed that the wall behind the man was covered by a large muslin curtain spanning its entire breadth.

"Ladies and gentlemen—thank you all for being here," Ravener began. "I'm very grateful. I also hope you've had a chance to look at some of the new pieces of bird art I've acquired. As you know, part of my name—Ravener—is a bird's name. So maybe that's the reason I'm so fond of the creatures."

He paused to study the crowd, making certain of its full attention. "I have two announcements to make. The first is that in a few weeks I will be marrying the most wonderful woman in the world. . . ."

There was a sudden murmur from the room.

"By great coincidence," he went on, relishing the moment, "she happens to be in this gallery tonight. In fact, she *owns* the gallery. Ladies and gentlemen, let me introduce my fiancée, Ariel McKenzie!"

The room erupted in applause. As Lorelei and Jon joined in, Jon glanced in the direction of Myles Coleridge and his wife. Coleridge was applauding, too. In contrast, the woman's hands never let go of the champagne flute she held; instead, the fingers gripped the glass with tensile strength.

Ariel McKenzie, for her part, stepped up beside Brian Ravener, blew several kisses to the audience, then kissed him on the cheek.

When the crowd quieted, she said, "Thank you—thank you, everyone. I know Brian has told some of you that he's a changed man because of me. But if you know Brian, you know nobody can change him—and there's nothing I would *want* to change."

"Bless you, darling," Ravener said, embracing her and pulling her to him in a gesture that appeared to startle her.

"The second announcement is this," Ravener went on, his voice rising now, commanding absolute attention to his words. "One thing many of you know about me is that I'm never satisfied. If it wasn't enough to capture this bird of paradise beside me, I've also come into possession of four other birds. In their own way, they're as beautiful. And a lot older than Ariel, besides. In a moment, you will meet them all."

He paused, savoring the suspense he had instilled.

"Audubon . . ." the man went on, "John James Audubon. Naturalist, explorer, author, publisher, entrepreneur, environmentalist—and certainly one of the most famous painters of birds who ever lived. When he was roaming North America in the first half of the nineteenth century, his ambition was to depict every one of the six hundred fifty bird species that existed on the continent at that time.

"Of that number, he completed paintings of only five hundred. The birds he never saw—and never painted—were those that made their habitat west of the Rocky Mountains and along the Pacific Coast. And why? Because history records that

Audubon never crossed the Rockies, never traveled on to the Pacific. . . ."

Ravener's voice thundered out across the room. "My friends—history is *wrong!* Through circumstances I cannot reveal, I recently became the owner of four extraordinary watercolors by Audubon himself—paintings of Western birds that no one knew existed—as well as documented proof that Audubon *did* travel west across the Rockies and *did* reach the Pacific Coast!"

Jon was aware that Lorelei had cast a sidelong glance in his direction, eager to know his response. The truth was, Jon was stunned. If documents proved that Audubon *had* reached the Pacific, *and* if the watercolors were authentic, their discovery was remarkable, revising everything that had been known about one of America's most celebrated artists.

Meanwhile, Ariel had stepped down from the platform and moved to one side of the muslin curtain covering the wall behind them. A young woman who appeared to be a gallery assistant stood at the other side.

"And what do I call these four Audubon watercolors that will now go into my personal collection?" Ravener exclaimed. "Let me present what I call—'The Audubon Quartet'!"

At Ravener's signal, Ariel and the assistant pulled away the curtain. There was a collective gasp of wonder from the crowd. Placed side by side were four watercolor paintings, each of a different bird, that bore the distinct characteristics of the master's work: the bright colors, the sharp outlines, the dramatic placement of the birds in their natural surroundings. The paintings were large, measuring more than three feet high and two feet wide. Each was framed and under protective glass.

Ravener stepped to the side, half-turning and gesturing in

their direction. "From left to right," he said, "they are the sage sparrow, Lawrence's goldfinch, the Montezuma quail, and a spotted owl feasting on a mole. Each painting has been authenticated by experts and its provenance determined without doubt."

He added with a grin, "And for any of you who are skeptical, I also have a letter dated 1843, written and signed by Audubon himself, in which he describes his journey overland to the Pacific and his travels down the coast."

Ravener looked out at the crowd, trying unsuccessfully to mask his triumph. At the same time, Jon noticed that Abel Lasher had worked his way to the row of people nearest Ravener and was staring past him to the watercolors on the wall.

"I'll admit I paid a pretty penny for the four of them . . ." Ravener was saying.

"How many pennies?" someone called out.

"More than the nine dollars and change Audubon's widow got for each of his other paintings when she sold them," Ravener called back.

There was laughter from the room.

"They're fake." The voice stopped the laughter like a pistol shot.

Ravener stepped forward on the platform, his eyes glowering. "Who said that?" he demanded.

"I did."

It was Abel Lasher. He stood staring up at Brian Ravener, a stubby finger thrust in the direction of the wall.

"Anyone who knows birds," Lasher told him, "knows that the Montezuma quail is also called the 'fool's quail.' And no one but a fool could have bought that painting and believed it was the real thing."

Throats cleared around the room and heads craned to get a better view. The two men stood facing one another. Ravener, at the front edge of the platform, glared down at Lasher with an expression of astonishment and rage.

"Shut up, Lasher!" someone in the room called. Jon knew it was Diana Cardigan.

Instead, Lasher again thrust out a finger, this time at the portrait of the goldfinch. "That goldfinch," he challenged. "I've seen better work in a third-grade art appreciation class."

By now, Ariel McKenzie had stepped back onto the platform, her face ashen. "Sir—this is a party. It's a *happy* time."

But Ravener was in no mood for conciliation. "Get out of here!" he shouted down at Lasher. "Get out now!"

Instead, Lasher stepped onto the platform. He was about to touch the painting of the owl when Ravener reached out a hand to Lasher's chest and shoved the man with force off the platform, in the direction of a side wall.

Momentarily airborne, Lasher slammed against the wall and fell sprawling, at the same time toppling a terra cotta sculpture of a dove, which smashed to pieces on the floor.

"Get out!" Ravener roared down at him.

"I'm bringing charges for assault!" The man struggled to his feet, then fell again. "I'll sue!"

"I'll kill you first!"

The next instant, Ravener was off the platform. He seized Lasher by the wrists and yanked him up. "Get out! You stinking little—!"

"Stop it! Stop it!" Ariel reached them, pulling at them, sobbing.

Ravener threw his hands up. Free of his attacker, Lasher

used the moment to escape. He swung an arm in the direction of the crowd. People gasped; those nearest Lasher drew back.

At once, the man plunged forward through the sea of startled faces, disappeared into the front room of the gallery and out into the night.

2

THE LATE FERRY, vehicles and passengers aboard, was underway soon after she arrived.

The passenger compartment was fuller than usual for the last boat of the night; the number added to, Jon guessed, by those with airline reservations, for whom the weather had demanded rearrangement of their plans. Still, he and Lorelei found seats next to a set of windows that looked out on a narrow deck. As they sat down, Jon saw that rivulets of windblown rain ran down the outside of the glass.

The rain had begun as they left the gallery. After the confrontation between Ravener and Lasher, the reception had come to an immediate and awkward end. Ariel McKenzie had fled in tears to a rear office. Ravener had rushed to comfort her, leaving the reception-goers at a loss for what to do. Most simply headed for the door, some carrying their champagne glasses with them as they went. Jon and Lorelei had remained, saying their polite good-byes to Ravener. He had responded manfully, but it was apparent that he was distracted and upset.

As the ship proceeded slowly toward Nantucket Sound,

people continued to move up and down the aisle. Some of them Jon recognized from the reception, including Diana Cardigan and her photographer.

There were also two men whom he assumed had been there. One was Wilson Tyne, a short man with rimless glasses, who was the director of a small, private art museum in Connecticut. The other man was taller, noticeably thin, with pale skin and white-blond hair. His name was David Bethune. He was an artist of some reputation, who had earned recognition with his paintings of female nudes.

The ship began to gather speed. On the port side, barely visible, Jon saw the lighthouse at Brant Point blinking a farewell. Unseen were the twin stone jetties at the entrance to the harbor. Soon the ferry would be in Nantucket Sound.

Lorelei supressed a yawn. "What time is it?" she asked. Jon looked at his watch. "Ten fifteen. We're running late. The weather probably."

Another yawn, which this time Lorelei allowed. "Do you mind if I try to nap some?"

"Go ahead. It's been a long day. And it won't be until after midnight that we'll reach Hyannis."

"Wake me when we get there." Lorelei removed her shoes and tucked her legs beneath her. Then she leaned her head against the seatback. In a moment, she was fast asleep.

Idly, Jon turned his gaze again in the direction of the windows. Beyond them, there was very little visible. An overhanging yellow light gave dim illumination to the deck itself, but he could see nothing of the rolling sea past the deck railing.

Under the circumstances, he decided that a nap might be a very good idea. He put his head against the seat and closed his eyes, feeling the broad swells of the open water rock the ship.

Soon he too was asleep.

"LORELEI, JON . . . MAY I join you?"

The voice woke him suddenly. Jon opened his eyes. Above him was the face of Brian Ravener.

"Excuse me . . . I'm sorry," Ravener apologized.

The man stood in the aisle next to them. Under his raincoat, he was still dressed in a tuxedo. The collar of the shirt was open and the bow tie gone.

"I'm sorry, really," he repeated. "I saw you from the back. I didn't know you were asleep."

By now, Lorelei had stirred. "Hi, Brian. Come and sit with us." She gestured to the empty seat that faced them.

"Thanks." Ravener slid into the seat. "Most of the other people on the ship pretend not to notice me." He frowned. "Not that I blame them after what happened at the gallery. Anyway, I thought I saw the light at Point Gammon, so the voyage should be over in a while."

"How much longer, do you think?" Lorelei asked.

"Another half hour, give or take," Ravener said, turning to her. At once, his face showed his concern. "Lorelei . . . what's wrong?"

When Jon looked, he saw her face was pale.

"Call me Captain Uncourageous, but I'm not the world's greatest sailor," she confessed.

"Would you like me to go back to the snack bar and get you something?" Jon suggested.

"I'll do it," she said. "Being on my feet might help."

She stood and stepped past Jon into the aisle. Somewhat unsteadily, she headed back along it, putting a hand against a wall as the ship rolled.

"Lorelei's a lovely woman," Ravener commented. "How long have you two known each other?"

"Several years," Jon told him. "She moved to Scarborough from New York City after a divorce. She was at loose ends, used whatever money she had to buy an antiques shop in Scarborough, and made it a success. We became friends soon after she arrived."

Ravener smiled. "I'm glad. You were pretty much at loose ends yourself for the years after your wife died."

"I guess I was," Jon agreed.

"Where will you be tonight? You're not driving back to Scarborough, I hope."

"No. We're staying on the Cape. The Osterville Inn. Tomorrow morning we'll be driving up to Boston."

"Really? Why didn't you tell me? I'll be in Boston also. Come for dinner, both of you."

"Thanks," Jon said. "To be honest, I didn't expect to see you on the boat. I thought you'd be at your Nantucket house."

"I would, normally," Ravener admitted. "But I'm riding shotgun on the Audubons."

"What do you mean?"

"At the moment, the paintings are belowdeck in an armored truck being watched over by the steely eyes of two armed guards. This morning I personally took them from the storage vault in my Boston house and oversaw the loading of them in the truck. My driver and I followed the truck from Boston to Hyannis, and I came over with them on the early boat. I had the paintings brought directly to the gallery and supervised their hanging. During the day, one or the other of the guards remained with them in the gallery.

"That's why I *know* those paintings can't be forgeries." His voice rose. "From the first day I acquired them, those Audubons have had the best protection anyone could give them. Lasher was dead wrong to call them fakes!"

He leaned back on the seat and sighed. "But of course that doesn't excuse the way I acted when he challenged them. I have a quick temper, too quick for my own good. What makes it worse is how much the whole rotten business upset Ariel. She was looking forward to tonight as such a joyful occasion. I'm sorrier than I can say for letting the event get out of hand."

He shook his head and sighed again. The apology had been sincere and deeply felt—not easy for a man as proud as Brian Ravener.

"Put it behind you," Jon said. "Under the circumstances, lots of people would have reacted the same way."

Ravener's eyes studied Jon. "Maybe," he admitted.

They were interrupted by Lorelei's return. She was carrying a paper cup.

Ravener saw her before Jon did. "Let me slip out," he said. "It'll be easier for you if I step into the aisle."

"Thank you," Lorelei said, moving to resume her seat beside the window.

Jon swung aside to let her pass. When he turned back, he saw that Ravener was still standing in the aisle, but now looking toward the windows and the deck beyond. His mouth opened and closed briefly. He seemed stricken.

"Brian, what is it?" Jon asked.

"Nothing. Not a thing." Ravener shifted his gaze from the

windows, looking back at them again. "Maybe I'll get something from the snack bar, too," he told them quickly.

Then he hurried off along the aisle.

Lorelei called after him. "Brian, the snack bar—"

But Ravener had disappeared.

She glanced at Jon and shrugged. "I was going to tell him the snack bar is closed."

"How did you get that?" Jon pointed to the paper cup.

"I ran into the purser. He found some Dramamine, then gave me the cup and told me where the water fountain is." She drained the cup.

As she did, Jon stepped into the aisle. "Before we get to port," he said, "I think I'll take a walk around the ship to stretch my legs."

She nodded. "Go ahead."

Jon started in the direction of the stern, taking the same route Ravener had. Passing the snack bar, he saw a "Closed" sign sitting prominently on the countertop. The lone counterman was locking the refrigerator for the night.

The ship slowed and began to alter course, swinging gradually to starboard. Jon continued past the snack bar, moving forward toward the bow again. As he walked, he looked briefly at the windows along the port side and noticed that the rain had stopped.

Then, in the low light of the narrow deck beyond, he saw two figures. The taller figure was in silhouette, so Jon couldn't see the face. He could see, though, that words were being exchanged between the two.

The shorter figure backed away. Under the light, Jon saw that it was Abel Lasher.

Abruptly, Lasher turned and walked away.

The other figure started after him. To Jon's surprise, he realized the person Lasher had been speaking with was Brian Ravener.

Then both were gone.

"PASSENGERS WITH VEHICLES should return to the main deck." The voice that crackled from the loudspeaker sounded weary.

Understandably, thought Jon as he shifted in his seat. It was well after midnight when the ferry slipped between the channel buoys and began to make her way into Hyannis Harbor.

Beside him, Lorelei watched the lights of the marina coming into view. "How long do we have?" she asked.

"Ten minutes or so. They have to off-load the cars and trucks first. We might as well wait here."

"Actually, I'd like a breath of air," she said. "Do you mind if I go out on deck?"

"I'll join you."

They rose and walked along the aisle to a steel door leading to the foredeck. Jon opened it and they stepped out. Directly opposite, there was the silhouette of a woman standing by herself against the rail. It was Diana Cardigan. As they approached, she turned.

"Snug harbor," she announced. "And none too soon. Another hour on the bounding main and my mal de mer would have kicked in. By the way, Pesky Swift and I are taking a taxi to the airport. Want to share it?"

"Thanks," Jon said, "but we're staying on the Cape tonight."

"So are we," the woman said. "We're booked into a motel

next to the airport. Separate rooms, of course. I'm not turned on by the idea of sleeping with a paparazzi wannabe. Besides, seeing Abel Lasher tonight will probably make me wake up screaming."

She paused and looked at them. "So what did you think of Ravener's Nantucket shindig? Lasher was certainly the skunk at the garden party, wasn't he?"

"I'm sorry for the way the evening ended," Jon acknowledged. "Most of all, for Brian's sake."

"I just wish Ravener had finished the job," Diana Cardigan said. "Kill Lasher, I mean. If it had been me, I would have."

A horn bellowed from the bridge of the ship, a signal they were about to dock.

The woman stepped back from the rail. "Excuse me, but I better locate Pesky, or no girl in Hyannis will be safe tonight."

She left the deck.

A short time later, the ferry was secured in her berth and Jon and Lorelei joined the other passengers who had begun to leave the ship.

Jon caught a glimpse of Wilson Tyne and David Bethune standing ahead of them in line. Under the bright lights that illuminated the docking area, the artist's epicene face looked even paler than before.

Then Jon noticed Bethune's left hand. On the back of it, from the wrist to the first knuckles, there were two bloody scratches, as if freshly made.

Jon was distracted by a loud metallic scraping sound: the portable stairway was being wheeled toward the ship. The gangway was swung across, and the line of people started toward it. As he and Lorelei reached the stairway, he discovered that the metal steps were slippery from the rain.

He took Lorelei's hand. But she had halted and was pointing down beyond the ship to the open area beyond the pilings where unloading operations had begun.

"Jon, look! It's Brian."

Jon saw him, too.

As vehicles emerged from the cavernous opening at the stern of the ship and rolled slowly down the ramp, Brian Ravener was dashing in and out among them, running away from the ship.

From the time Jon had seen him and Lasher together on the deck, more than a half hour earlier, Ravener had not returned to join them.

As the line of disembarking cars and trucks made its way onto the asphalt, Jon noticed a Brinks armored truck. It proceeded toward the terminal, then turned left and headed toward the exit gates.

Ravener, on the other hand, continued running straight ahead.

At that moment, a black limousine appeared swiftly from the shadows. It drew alongside Ravener, who halted, gasping. The limousine stopped. The window on the driver's side was lowered. Ravener wrenched open a rear door of the car and leaped in. The door slammed shut.

The vehicle sprang forward, gaining speed again, and turned into the street beyond.

3

"JON, I NEED your help."

No greeting. No preamble. Nothing more.

"Brian, is that you? What's wrong?"

"It's me. And plenty's wrong."

A pause. "Hold on," Ravener resumed. "There are some men coming to the house."

Jon held the phone with one hand. With the other, he took a sip of coffee from a plastic cup. He had left Lorelei asleep in their room and come down to the office of the inn to get some coffee from the breakfast bar. As he was pouring it, the desk clerk had seen him and signaled that there was a call for him. Puzzled, Jon had gone over to the telephone and taken it.

Ravener's voice came back on the line. "You'll be in Boston today? That's what you said."

"Yes. We'll be arriving about noon."

"Good. I'll be with my attorneys in the afternoon. But I still hope you and Lorelei can come for dinner."

"Certainly, but why—"

"Abel Lasher's dead."

"What!"

"They found his body floating in Nantucket Sound at dawn. The police think he was murdered. Also, that I killed him."

"Did they tell you that?

"They didn't have to. The men who just arrived . . . they're homicide detectives. They've come, as they put it in the subtle way detectives have, to 'talk with me.' Someone obviously told them about the fight Lasher and I had yesterday." He added, "And my threat to kill him."

"Then are you sure you want Lorelei and me there tonight?"

"Absolutely," Ravener insisted. "Right now you're among the few people I *want* to talk with. Make it at seven."

"All right. We'll be there."

"I'm counting on it."

The phone went dead.

LIKE MANY OF its neighbors, Brian Ravener's house was a beautifully preserved brick structure, built in the Federal style more than a century earlier. A wrought-iron gas lamp, now electrified, stood close to the stone steps that led to the front door.

As Jon and Lorelei went up the walk, Jon scanned the tall windows facing the street. Draperies were drawn across them. The front door of the house was of polished oak, with a brass knocker and an oval plaque below it on which the name "Ravener" was engraved in ornate script.

Jon lifted the knocker, rapped, and let it fall. There was a slight scrapping noise from the far side of the door. A glint of light showed through a tiny peephole.

"Mr. Wilder?" a woman's voice asked.

"Good evening, Mrs. Ferris," he replied.

The door was opened a few inches by a short, plump woman in a gray housekeeper's uniform.

"Excuse the wait, sir," she apologized, "but Mr. Ravener asked me to check everyone who comes to the door. He's had lots of visitors today." She frowned. "He's in the parlor," she added, opening the door for them to enter.

"I'm here, Mrs. Ferris," Brian Ravener said. He stood at the other end of the foyer. "Jon, Lorelei, good evening. At least let's hope it's better than the day has been. Come in."

Ravener led them to a nearby room that served as a parlor. As Jon had noticed from the street, the draperies were drawn.

"Have a seat," Ravener said, motioning to a set of chairs. As they sat down, Ravener's eyes moved past them to the door. "Please join us, darling."

Jon turned. In the doorway stood Ariel McKenzie. She wore a pale blue-silk dress, and her dark hair fell loosely around her shoulders.

"Good evening, Mrs. Merriwell . . . Mr. Wilder." Her voice had the same Southern softness Jon recalled. "Except for the circumstances, it's a pleasure to see both of you again."

Somewhere in the house, a telephone began to ring.

"The damn thing's been ringing all day long," Ravener groused. "Mostly, it's the media. One reporter even asked me if the Audubon Quartet was some kind of music group."

He turned and left the room. As he did, Ariel's eyes followed him. "Poor Brian," she said. "Today has been so difficult for him. Anybody who knows him knows he couldn't hurt a flea."

"I'm sure it means a lot to him to have you here," Lorelei assured her.

Ravener reentered, his face grim. "That call was from my lawyer," he told them. "There'll be something on the late news about Lasher's murder. He said my name will come up."

"Oh, dear. In what way?" Ariel asked him, alarmed.

His eyes swung to her. "In what way do you imagine? As the one who killed him."

THROUGHOUT DINNER, RAVENER was taciturn despite the splendid meal Mrs. Ferris had prepared, as well as the French pinot noir he had taken from his private stock and poured liberally. Only when the subject of his and Ariel's impending wedding was raised did he relax at all, contributing a few details of their plans.

"You said you hope to have an August ceremony," Lorelei remarked. "Have you set a date?"

"Sometime in the second week," Ariel said. "And as Brian mentioned, it'll be at his house on the island. August in Nantucket is a horrid month, what with the tourists. But Brian's so busy for the next six weeks, he couldn't take the time."

"You'll keep both houses, I imagine," Jon said. "This one and the Nantucket house."

"Yes," Ravener responded. "But we'll sell Ariel's. Right now she's living in a little carriage house on Hussey Street. A charming place, and close to the center of town. We'll get a lot for it, I'm sure."

"Thank goodness, Brian has a head for business," Ariel said, placing her hand gently over his. "But what most people don't know is that he's also a most romantic man. When we became engaged, he surprised me with a white BMW convertible. He told me the initials stood for Be My Wife."

"Ariel is a lovely name," Lorelei said. "Wasn't she the good spirit in *The Tempest*?"

The woman nodded. "Daddy was the one who named me. He loved Shakespeare and the classics. He was a Southern gentleman in every way, and a true son of Savannah."

"Did you grow up in Savannah?" Jon inquired.

"Yes, and was schooled there," Ariel said, "beginning with Miss Wellhammer's Academy. After that, a junior college for young ladies, so refined it offered courses in cotillion etiquette. Then, very much against my daddy's wishes, I came north to Yankee country."

"And, I suspect, you met some very improper Bostonians," Ravener put in.

"But enough about me," she continued, looking now at Jon. "What brought you to Boston, Jon? Was it the birds?"

"In a way," he confessed. "Ever since I can remember, I've wanted to ride a swan boat in the Public Garden. This afternoon I finally got my wish."

Ravener smiled for the first time. "Who would believe it? Jon Wilder, respected bird artist and ornithologist, comes all the way to Boston to ride a swan boat in the park."

During dessert and coffee, Ravener attempted to maintain a bonhomie. But Jon sensed turbulent emotions beneath it that the man was struggling to overcome.

The dessert plates had been cleared and a second round of coffee poured when Ravener turned to Ariel, who sat beside him. "My dear," he suggested in a casual voice, "why don't you take Lorelei on a tour of the house?"

She looked at him uncertainly, then nodded. "Well, if you think this is a good time for it."

"I do," he said.

Ariel rose from the table, as did Lorelei.

"Come with me," Ariel said and led Lorelei from the room. Soon the sounds of their conversation faded and footsteps on the stairway could be heard.

"Ariel is a delightful woman," Jon told Ravener.

"Yes, I'm very lucky," Ravener agreed. But his mind was obviously on matters other than the virtues of his fiancée. "Let's go into the library. I prefer that we talk there."

THE LIBRARY OF Ravener's townhouse was a large, high-ceilinged room, paneled in mahogany, that looked out on a courtyard and garden at the rear. One wall contained bookshelves; the others were hung with a variety of paintings, many of them by Americans, including oils by Copley, Eakins, and Cassatt. On the mantle of the marble fireplace a French clock chimed nine times, then resumed its muted ticking in the silence that had filled the room since they arrived.

Ravener guided Jon to a leather-covered wing chair. He pulled up another opposite.

"I'm afraid," he said. His face had a beseeching look that Jon had never seen before. "I'm afraid," he repeated. "I admit it. Listen to this . . ."

He reached to a side table where a copy of the *Boston Herald* lay. He picked it up and read:

> " 'The body of Abel Lasher, founder and editor of *Art Now* magazine, was discovered early this morning in Nantucket Sound, near Yarmouthport, by a commercial fishing boat. Preliminary autopsy reports suggest the victim drowned. Lasher, who was known for his

brusque manner and acerbic critiques of artists and their works, had been on Nantucket for an art reception, according to a source . . .' "

He held the newspaper toward Jon. "Would you like to read the rest?"

"Not really."

"Then I'll spare you the details." Ravener tossed the newspaper aside and stood. "Jon, I need your help. You're an artist. You know the profession—other artists, dealers, the collectors."

"Maybe," Jon said. "But what I'm not is a detective."

"I'm not asking that," Ravener said. "What I need is someone with your special knowledge of the arts—in particular, of the works of Audubon."

Ravener walked to a sideboard where a Baccarat crystal decanter sat. He seized it and began pouring brandy into a large snifter. "Some for you?" he asked Jon over his shoulder as he poured.

"No, thanks."

Jon paused. "Last night on the ferry, before we reached Hyannis, you came and sat with Lorelei and me."

Ravener swirled the snifter, tested it, then sipped. "I remember," he said. "Yes."

"Lorelei felt queasy, so she went back to the snack bar. A short time after that, you did the same."

"That's right. I got myself some orange juice, as I recall. What does that have to do with anything?"

"When Lorelei returned, she told me that she'd found the snack bar closed."

Ravener again swirled the snifter, studying the rich amber liquid as it moved languidly around the glass.

"Yes, you're right," he acknowledged finally. "The snack bar was closed. The reason I left you and Lorelei was that I suddenly saw Abel Lasher on the deck. It sounds ridiculous to say it, but I felt I had to talk with him."

"About what?"

"I wanted to apologize for shoving him. That also sounds ridiculous, but it's the truth."

"What happened?"

"When I went out to where I'd seen him on the deck, he wasn't there. I decided to walk around until I found him. I think Lasher had been looking for a place to smoke a cigarette out of the rain."

"And you found him," Jon said.

"Yes. I called his name. When he saw me, I approached him. I told him I was sorry for what had happened at the gallery, and asked if we could talk. Instead, he turned his back on me and walked away. I started after him, but he just disappeared. By then, I was upset all over again, so I stayed out on deck a while by myself until I cooled off. It wasn't something I could explain to you and Lorelei. That's why I never returned."

"I see."

Ravener regarded him. "You see what exactly?"

"Frankly, I don't know," Jon admitted. "I told you, I'm not a detective. I'm not even sure of what questions I should ask."

"Well, I had the pleasure of talking with the police earlier. So I'll give you their questions and my answers. Question: 'Mr. Ravener, were you alone on deck for the remainder of the trip?' My answer: 'Yes.' Question: 'What did you do, sir, after the boat got to Hyannis?' Answer: 'Gentlemen'—I called them gentlemen—'I drove with the armored car here to my house and put the paintings back into the vault.' "

"You drove back with the armored car?" Jon asked.

"Yes. Why?"

"Because after the ferry docked, Lorelei and I had just reached the outside steps. We saw you running toward the parking lot; you were picked up by a limousine, while the armored car continued toward the exit gate."

Ravener looked flustered. "Uh . . . well, yes. I did. When I told you I drove with the truck, I meant I accompanied it in my limousine. My driver had been waiting at the terminal to pick me up. We'd agreed to meet the truck on the street around the corner from the terminal. Because it was so late, I ran to find the car. I wanted to get on the road as soon as possible."

There was a hesitancy in the man's voice that made the explanation sound sincere. Jon hoped it was true.

"When you were interviewed by the police," he asked, "did you mention anyone whom you thought might be the murderer?"

"Any *one*? I could have handed them a phone book; Lasher had that many enemies! But yes, I gave them names. I also said I was convinced that the murderer was at the reception and, of course, on the late ferry coming back. The person who killed Lasher knew he would be on the ship; he confronted him on deck and after he killed him, tossed the body overboard."

"There was a fairly heavy sea last night," Jon suggested. "Maybe Lasher lost his balance and fell over the rail."

"Unlikely. Lasher had the survival instincts of a cockroach. He'd throw somebody else overboard to save his own life, if it came to that."

Ravener stopped his pacing and looked down at Jon. "And there's one thing the newspaper got wrong. Lasher didn't die from drowning. He was strangled."

"How do you know that?"

"I have a friend who's close to the police commissioner. He made a few discreet inquiries. The preliminary autopsy shows the cause of death as strangulation."

Ravener turned to the tall windows facing out on the rear courtyard, now in darkness. When he spoke, it was with deep feeling, his voice low.

"The summer that you and I met," he said. "Do you remember it?"

"Of course. The beach near Truro. I was swimming in the ocean and got swept out by the undertow. You saved my life."

"Now I'm the one caught in the undertow, Jon. And I need you to save me. This whole business is dragging me into deeper water than I can deal with alone."

Jon rose. "Then I guess it's my turn, isn't it? I'll do what I can." He offered out a hand to Ravener.

"Thank you," Ravener said quietly. He clasped Jon's hand in both of his. "And I'll do everything I can to give you what you need. Just tell me."

"First," Jon said, "I'd like to see the Audubon Quartet. You said you have the paintings in your vault."

"Come on. I'll take you there."

They left the library and returned along a central hall. Ravener guided Jon into the large kitchen and to what appeared to be a set of pantry shelves. Swung aside, the shelves revealed a steel-clad door. Ravener unlocked the door and opened it. Beyond it was a narrow stairway leading down. He switched on a light, then descended, with Jon several steps behind.

"As I said, the Audubons were brought here last night by the armored truck," Ravener continued. "And I personally returned them to the vault."

"Before the paintings traveled to Nantucket," Jon asked, "did you show them to anyone?"

"To a few people, yes. Wilson Tyne was one."

Jon was surprised. "Tyne? The museum director?"

"He's also an expert on the works of Audubon. He was suggested by the dealer from whom I bought them."

"Who was the dealer?

"Duncan Rutledge, in New York."

"Did you show them to anybody else?"

Ravener thought for a moment. "Two others, actually. One was Diana Cardigan. She'd heard a rumor that I'd bought the paintings and contacted me. She told me that *Au Courant* would like to do a piece concerning them. Two weeks ago, she flew to Boston and I showed her the paintings. Her photographer also took some pictures."

"Was it the same photographer who was with her at the gallery?"

"As a matter of fact, yes."

At the base of the stairs, Ravener switched on another light. Opposite them was a second steel door with an electronic keypad beside it. Tapping out a set of numbers on the pad, he waited until a small light glowed green. Then he opened the door.

Beyond it was a room that became illuminated as they entered. Against the far wall was an arrangement of metal boxes, many of them large and flat. Near the door were several thermostats and dials that Jon guessed controlled the room's temperature and humidity. In the center of the room, a wooden table stood.

Ravener withdrew one of the boxes from the wall and placed it on the table. "I keep the Audubons in here," he said.

From the box he carefully removed four large sheets of watercolor paper, each separated by a protective covering, and placed them on the table. He moved the box to one side and began laying out the sheets side by side, noting each one as he did.

"The Montezuma quail . . . Lawrence's goldfinch . . . The spotted owl . . . and the sage sparrow—or what Audubon identifies on the painting as "The Desert Sparrow.' "

Jon leaned forward for a closer look.

"Well?" Ravener asked finally.

Jon glanced up. "You say Duncan Rutledge was the dealer who sold these to you?"

"Yes. Officially, it was his firm. Granby and Rutledge. They're as respectable as you can get."

"And Rutledge had a look at them himself?"

"Of course."

Jon examined the painting of the goldfinch. The small bird, seated on an alder branch, displayed a black face and chin, a yellow breast, and bright yellow patches on its wings.

"Did Rutledge offer any comments on the materials, or the technique?" Jon asked.

"No. None. He admired them, certainly. He told me I was extremely lucky to have acquired them. Why do you ask?"

Jon pointed to the watercolor of the finch. "The Lawrence's goldfinch. Look at the wing coverts. Do you notice anything unusual about the gold?"

Ravener examined the painting closely. "It has a certain sheen. I can see that."

"More than is typical of Audubon," Jon said. "The reason is the use of gold metallic paint. From everything we know, Audubon experimented with gold paint on only three works, all done about 1825. In two of them, the paint discolored due to oxidation. Audubon was understandably displeased with the results."

"You mean he didn't use gold metallic paint after that?"

"I doubt it very much," Jon said. "Especially for paintings done late in his career."

Brian Ravener grew pale. He continued staring at the portrait of the finch. Several times he shook his head, as if to disallow the thought that had begun to fill his mind.

"Were any chemical tests done on these paintings?" Jon asked at last.

Ravener straightened and shook his head again. "Rutledge and the experts, Tyne included, were so sure they were authentic, nobody suggested it. They didn't think there was a need."

His eyes took on a stricken look. "But what you're saying . . . is that what Lasher claimed was right? These paintings are forgeries?"

"I'm afraid so," Jon said simply.

"My God!" Ravener turned desperately in Jon's direction. "If that's true, what happened to the real Audubon Quartet? Who stole it? And where is it now?"

Jon said nothing. Other questions, dark ones, came to mind. Was there, in fact, a real Audubon Quartet? Or was this all a hoax in which Jon was being made an unwitting participant? Worse—was it a hoax that Brian Ravener himself had planned?

4

SUNLIGHT DAPPLING THE surface of the sound, great cumulus clouds building over the twin forks of Long Island miles to the south, a flock of mallards flying low along the beach—it was a view Jon never tired of.

That morning he and Lorelei had driven down from Boston. He'd taken her to her house, then headed home. Now he sat in the Range Rover in the turnaround area outside the garage and looked at the house. Built of native fieldstone, it stood three stories tall. At one end was a turret where, on the second floor, Jon had his studio. From that studio came the bird paintings sought by collectors, as well as those works that illustrated a series of nature guides to birds.

The house stood on a remote stretch of land called Plover Point, on the southeastern coast of Connecticut. At the far side of the house were a stone terrace and a lawn, beyond which was a beach bordering the broad expanse of Seal Island Sound. Years ago, when he and his young wife had bought the house, it was the panoramic view that had attracted them the most.

But this was not the time to linger and appreciate it; he had work to do.

Jon stepped down from the car, retrieved his overnight case, and walked through the garage into the house. He went immediately to his study.

On his answering machine he found a message from Brian Ravener. The man repeated his gratitude for Jon and Lorelei's visit of the night before. He also assured Jon there would be some "interesting material," as he put it, that he would send to Jon within the week. Jon made a note of the message, then turned to the shelves of books beside his desk.

He quickly found what he was looking for. It was the first of a five-volume set entitled *Ornithological Biography,* by John James Audubon. The lengthy work was, in fact, Audubon's autobiography, written over a span of eight years and completed in 1839, when Audubon was fifty-four years old.

Most of the details of the man's life Jon knew by heart. Born in 1785, in what is now Haiti, Audubon was the son of a French sea captain and his Creole mistress. When she died several months after giving birth, Captain Audubon brought the baby with him to France to be raised by himself and his French wife. At twenty-one, the young Audubon emigrated to the United States, some say to avoid conscription in the French Army. He settled in the Philadelphia area, married, and then moved west into the Kentucky and Missouri Territories, where he worked at a variety of mercantile trades.

But having studied art in France, Audubon also turned his attention to a subject that fascinated him and that would become the passion of his life—the birds. By the age of thirty-nine, he had drawn and painted so many species that he was able to secure a publisher for a collection he called *The Birds of America.*

Throughout his lifetime, the man displayed a boundless energy; much like Brian Ravener himself, Jon thought. The artist's spirit of adventure and his restless curiosity kept him on the move continually—from Labrador to the Florida Keys, the Gulf Coast, and westward to the foothills of the Rockies.

Still, it was in Europe that his genius was first recognized and where his reputation as an artist grew. On visits there, Audubon affected the dress and manner of an American frontiersman. With his remarkable good looks and flowing, shoulder-length hair, and dressed in buckskin and rough woodsman's garments, he seemed to European eyes the epitome of the spirit of a young America. His natural exuberance and sense of showmanship soon made him a much sought after celebrity in the salons of London and Paris, where, coincidentally, he sold a number of his works.

Yet his heart would always be with the adopted country he had come to love so well. In 1842, he purchased land on the West Side of Manhattan, overlooking the Hudson River, and built an estate that he called "Minnie's Land." It was there, in 1851, that he died at the age of sixty-six.

Jon put aside the book and took from a side pocket of his overnight case a manila envelope Ravener had given him last night. "What's in it?" Jon had asked. "You'll see," Ravener had told him, adding nothing more.

What the envelope contained was a photocopy of the letter Audubon had written in 1843 and that Ravener had acquired with his purchase of the Audubon Quartet itself.

As Ravener had noted when he unveiled the paintings, there

is nothing to suggest that Audubon ever traveled west beyond the Rocky Mountains. Rather, from April to August of 1843, it is assumed that Audubon spent five months at Fort Union in the Dakota Territory. What he did there was not specifically detailed. Was it possible that during those months, he *could* have traveled overland to the Pacific Coast?

Jon picked up the letter and began to read what he immediately recognized as Audubon's distinctive flowing script.

Addressed to his wife Lucy, it was dated August 16, 1843:

> *My Dearest Lucy,*
>
> *We have arrived at Fort Union after a most glorious journey west. The ocean of the Pacific, which I encountered at Puerto de San Francisco in the Republic of Mexico, is like nothing I have seen before. Viewing the Pacific, as her great waves dash over jagged rocks, our Atlantic Ocean appears very tame indeed. And here is all manner of Nature in profusion.*
>
> *Weary as my body is from the hardships of my travels, I take Delight in the birds I have seen in goodly numbers, many new to me and of remarkable Colour. As often as I could, I sketched and painted them until my fingers ached . . .*

The remainder of the letter provided an outline of the routes that Audubon had taken. Instead of traveling up the Missouri River to Fort Union, at what is now the North Dakota–Montana border, Audubon and his party had continued west from St. Louis, crossed the Colorado Rockies, skirted the Great Salt Lake, and arrived, finally, at San Francisco Bay. They ranged up and down the coast for several weeks, then headed east again, traversing the Northwest Territory and arriving at Fort Union in mid-August. In a tender postscript, Audubon expressed his eagerness to return to Minnie's Land, embrace Lucy and their sons, Jon and Victor, and in his words, "to take my Leisure with my family."

Jon put the pages to one side. It occurred to him again, as it had at the time of Ravener's announcement, that if the letter and the Audubon Quartet were genuine, the fact of their discovery would change all that had been known and published about Audubon.

The telephone jarred him from his reverie.

"Jon? Brian. I'm glad you're there," Ravener said. "Listen. I didn't mean to be so inscrutable last night about the information I'll be sending you. I've hired investigators to check the backgrounds of some people who might have murdered Lasher. People who were on that ferry coming back."

"Who did you ask them to check?" Jon inquired.

"Wilson Tyne and David Bethune, among others. Also, Diana Cardigan." He added, "And Jack Briscoe."

"Briscoe?" Jon was puzzled. "At the reception, he told Lorelei and me that he was staying at his beach house on the island. He even invited us to visit him."

"Maybe he changed his mind," Ravener said. "Anyway, I saw him on the vehicle deck of the ferry coming back. I'm sure it was Briscoe—beard, dark glasses, the gold chains. He was getting into a Jeep Cherokee."

"There were a lot of other people on that ferry," Jon reminded him. "Walk-on passengers, and some who might have stayed in their cars. One of them might have wanted to kill Lasher, too."

"True," Ravener agreed. "But those four had a particular dislike of him. I know that for a fact. Diana Cardigan told me as much when she visited my house. As for Briscoe and Bethune, Lasher had ridiculed their talents in the pages of his magazine. Why Tyne had a beef against Lasher, I'm not sure. But the night of the reception, I saw him and Lasher talking and Tyne was very angry about something."

"Okay," Jon said, "I'll speak with them and see what I can learn." He added, "By the way, I read the copy of Audubon's letter that you gave me last night."

"A remarkable document, isn't it?"

"But I'm curious about one thing," Jon said. "If someone had the opportunity to forge the paintings, couldn't they have also forged the letter?"

"Impossible," Ravener replied at once. "I kept the paintings in my house, as you know. But the letter wasn't with them. It was in the hands of my attorney. He was about to have the text authenticated by a handwriting expert, just to make sure it was genuine. Tests proved it was. When he took the letter my attorney held onto the original, but made several photocopies, one of which I gave to you.

"At any rate," Ravener continued, "I'll be sending the investigators' report as soon as I receive it."

"I'll give you a call when it arrives."

"Good. And again, I'm glad you and Lorelei could join us. Give her my best."

"I will. And mine to Ariel."

"I'll do that. Good-bye, Jon."

Ravener rang off.

As Jon hung up the phone, he heard the sound of a car approaching the house. It stopped in the turnaround area near the garage. A short time later, he heard a car door slam.

Going to the front windows, he recognized the auburn-haired woman coming up the walkway.

It was Meredith Coleridge.

As she continued along the walk, Jon went to the foyer. She had begun to climb the stone steps to the front door, when he opened it. If she was surprised by his sudden appearance, she didn't show it. Instead, she took a step back and regarded him before she spoke.

"Good afternoon, Mr. Wilder."

"Mrs. Coleridge . . ."

"Usually I have better manners than to show up on people's doorsteps unannounced. Forgive me."

She gave Jon the studied smile of a fashion model posing for a photograph. In fact, Jon thought, despite the simple blouse and skirt she wore, she had a model's aura of emotionless detachment.

"You do have time for us to talk." It was a statement, not a question.

"Certainly."

"Good." She looked up at the facade of the large, rambling house surrounded by tall trees. "It's an impressive place you have here."

"Thank you," Jon said. "But living alone, I sometimes think it's too much for one person."

Her hazel eyes regarded him. "I understand. I also know what it is to live alone in a large house."

From her expression, Jon decided to say nothing. He escorted her into the foyer and led her toward his study.

As they passed the kitchen, he asked, "Would you like anything to drink?"

"Ice water," she answered. "Please."

He brought her to the study and returned to the kitchen, where he fixed an iced tea for himself, then filled a glass with the remaining ice.

Ice water. It seemed appropriate that she should ask for it. It wasn't only her glacial, finely sculpted features. More than that, there seemed an icy countenance about her in which feelings played no part.

Entering the study with the glasses, he saw that she was studying a framed Audubon print of Carolina parakeets that was hanging on the wall beside the desk.

"The Audubon," she noted, gesturing. "It's from the Havell engravings for *The Birds of America.*"

"You know it, obviously," Jon said, handing her a glass.

"Myles has one also," Meredith Coleridge said. "What do you like about it in particular?"

"The antic spirit of the birds themselves," Jon told her. "And their brilliant colors—yellow, orange, green. It's one of the most festive paintings Audubon did.

"Unfortunately," he went on, "the species is extinct, killed off by poachers for the feathers, by farmers who thought of them as pests, and by so-called 'sportsmen,' who shot them when they wanted to kill something for the fun of it."

"Myles says that certain species bring about their own eradication through stupidity," she remarked, curious at Jon's response. "He'd say that if those parakeets hadn't been so innocent and trusting of human beings, they might have gone on to survive."

"Is that what you believe?" Jon asked.

She looked at him in silence. "Thank you for the water," she said, sipping at the glass.

She then began a slow circuit of the study, glancing at the other paintings on the walls. "Quite a collection you have here, Mr. Wilder."

Jon perched on a corner of his desk, saying nothing.

"As you know, art is a passion for my husband," she continued, "along with the accumulation of great wealth. What his other passions are, I couldn't say."

"Excuse me, Mrs. Coleridge," he said, "but you didn't come here to discuss either birds or art with me, I'm sure."

"No." She sank into a chair in the corner of the room. "Let me begin by asking you some questions."

"Go ahead."

"Will you help Brian prove his innocence?"

"I beg your pardon?" Startled, Jon set down his glass.

"I said, will you help prove that Brian Ravener did not kill Abel Lasher? I don't believe he's guilty. And I don't think you do. Am I right?"

"Yes," Jon said. "But other people do."

Her eyes narrowed. "Despite rumors to the contrary, I know he's not a murderer." She hesitated. "I was married to him years ago, as you may know. He's not the sort of man who'd do a thing like that."

"Why come to me? I'm not an investigator."

"What he needs most is someone like you, someone who knows his way around the art world, who can dig into its dark corners where investigators wouldn't think to look."

"If you wanted me to help him," Jon asked, "why didn't you just call me?"

"It wasn't something I could do over the telephone," she replied. "It was important to me that I talk with you directly, face to face."

"You make it sound like a job interview."

"It is," she said. "So will you help him?"

"Yes," he told her. "The truth is, Brian already asked me to and I said I would."

She bowed her head. "Thank you," she said. "I'm glad."

"Now let me ask you a few questions," he continued. "How did you find your way here? To my house, I mean. It's not exactly on the tourist maps."

"Myles told me."

"You asked him?"

Meredith Coleridge shook her head. "Myles and I were talking about you after the gallery reception. He was complimenting you as an artist; he said you painted seabirds particularly well, perhaps because you lived along the water. When I asked where, he told me the town was Scarborough, Connecticut. Since I was driving to New York this afternoon, I thought I'd stop. I found a gas station on the highway and asked the attendant if he knew you. He said yes, but that you liked your privacy, and that the townspeople never gave out your address. An excessively large tip for wiping the windshield changed his mind."

"Then your husband didn't come with you," Jon said.

"Myles had a late-morning meeting with some Wall Street people, so he took his plane. He's a pilot, you know. I decided to come over on the ferry instead and drive down."

"Have you both been on Nantucket since the weekend?"

"Yes. We have a house overlooking the harbor. When the weather's hot, I prefer it to our apartment in Manhattan, or our estate along the Hudson."

"I have another question," Jon went on. "Do you think the

paintings that were unveiled at the Wide Wharf Gallery are forgeries, as Lasher said?"

"I have no idea. Myles and I were at the far end of the room. We never had a chance to see them at close range."

She drained the glass, put it to one side, and stood. "It's getting late. I have a long drive to New York. Will you excuse me?"

"Certainly." Jon stood as well.

He guided her from the study and walked with her to the front foyer, opening the door.

But instead of leaving, she turned to him. "Thank you again for helping Brian."

Jon looked into the hazel eyes. "It matters to you, doesn't it, that Brian is proved innocent."

"Yes."

"Why?"

"It just does. Don't ask me the reasons." She turned and started down the steps to the front walk.

Jon watched her go. She moved swiftly without looking back, her heels clicking on the flagstone walk.

Don't ask me the reasons, she had told him.

But what were they?

Would he learn them?

And if so, would he be sorry that he had?

IT WAS MID-AFTERNOON when Jon drove into Scarborough. He bought some necessary groceries, refilled the gasoline tank in the Range Rover, and picked up the mail that had accumulated in his post-office box. Driving along Harbor Street, he parked near Lorelei's antiques shop and walked toward it. As he approached, he saw the shop was crowded. At the same moment, Lorelei saw him. She smiled, waved, then gave a shrug that said "I'd love to see you, but now isn't the time." He nodded and waved back, then started for his car.

"Jon!"

From the opposite side of the street, a stentorian voice boomed his name. Jon turned to see the great, bearded form of Colin Hightower emerging from the woodworking shop he owned.

Colin was dressed in a vast red-and-white-striped sports shirt that overlapped his khaki shorts, and which, given the man's voluminous proportions, presented the appearance of a beachside cabana supported by a pair of massive, hairy legs. In one hand Colin held the cane that assisted him in walking. In the other was a paper bag.

"Jon!" the man called again, and swung his cane in the air, beckoning to Jon.

Jon crossed the street to where his friend stood at the shop door. Hanging on the inside of the door was a sign announcing that Mr. Hightower was "Out to Lunch."

"It's three-thirty in the afternoon," Jon said. "Isn't it a little late for lunch?"

"It's not my lunch, dear boy," Colin announced in the rotund baritone that bore traces of his British roots. "It's the birds' lunch, if you will."

"The birds?"

"Hold this while I lock the door." Colin handed the bag to Jon, then delved into a pocket for his keys.

Jon held up the bag and looked at it. "It's not birdseed you've got in here. It's too heavy."

"No. The bag is filled with scones. Tea biscuits," Colin said. "Come with me to the harbor. I'll explain."

He started across the street in the direction of the harbor. Entering the small park that bordered it, they passed a set of swings and seesaws, all occupied with squealing children. On nearby benches, mothers talked among themselves.

They continued onto a brick walkway leading to a seawall at the harbor's edge. Halfway along the walk, Colin halted.

"Let's sit here." He moved to a wooden bench beside the walk and sat down with a force that rocked the bench.

Jon also sat down and then handed him the paper bag. "This time at least you're not feeding the birds year-old Girl Scout cookies you discovered in a drawer."

Colin opened the bag and looked inside. "No. These scones are far worse. If I'm caught in the act by the police, I'll be arrested on a charge of cruelty to animals. They were sent to me by a niece who lives in Manchester. Knowing I'm a connoisseur of tea, she thought I might enjoy them as an accompaniment. Nonetheless, I fear to say these scones are virtually inedible. I had to break them with a mallet, they're so hard."

Jon noticed gulls and terns had begun circling above. Colin raised his head and looked at them. "My breakfast guests are telling me they're hungry." He waved his cane in their direction. "Patience, my fine-feathered friends! Patience! In a moment, I will cast my scones upon the waters."

He went to the seawall, reached into the bag and began flinging pieces of the broken scones into the harbor. Jon joined him. Almost at once, more birds appeared, shrieking, wheeling, diving for the food. Jon could see at a distance a flock of mallards padding rapidly in their direction, attracted by the squawking and activity.

"I've heard from Lorelei about your Nantucket visit and all the misadventures that flowed from it," Colin said as he continued tossing hunks of broken scones. "Also, about your friend's request of you to find the killer of that critic. And suppose you do? If someone suspects you're asking pointed questions, then . . ." He left the sentence incomplete.

"I'd be putting myself at risk?"

Colin's answer was a grunt. He turned back to the seawall and resumed the feeding of the birds. Many more had gathered overhead, while still more continued to arrive by sea.

Jon now observed a cormorant farther out, almost to the harbor channel. The large, solitary bird ignored the noisy commotion at the seawall. Rather, it continued gliding on, imperiously unconcerned, its sleek black feathers glistening, its bill raised upward in a gesture of disdain.

Suddenly it thrust its long neck forward, plunged, and disappeared from sight. Colin obviously had been watching it as well.

"Take a lesson, Jon," he said at last. "As you know, some birds are mostly surface feeders, like these ducks. They're after easy pickings. You yourself could also pick up some tasty tidbits in your interviews. On the other hand, think of the cormorant that dives deep into the water and appears to stay below forever till it finds the thing it seeks."

Jon gave his friend a sidelong glance. "But deep water can get awfully murky and unfriendly."

"True," said Colin.

Then he waved a hand in the direction of the mallards that were feeding just below. "Still, if you're too visible," he went on, "you could well become a sitting duck."

5

THE EXPERIENCE WAS so reverential to Jon that he was almost inclined to genuflect. After climbing the stone steps leading to the front entrance of the Metropolitan Museum of Art, he paused inside the doors, letting his eyes travel up the massive columns that surrounded the great hall. In silence he gazed at the vaulted ceiling high above. Entering the Metropolitan Museum always gave him the same sense of awe and wonderment he felt on visiting a magnificent cathedral. Within it, and in spite of the crowds of visitors and tourists that swarmed through it, he felt a peace and blessedness, and a reassurance in the permanence of art.

He and Malachi La Tour had agreed to meet at eleven o'clock. It was ten minutes to the hour now, not time enough to wander through the galleries. Instead, he made his way across the hall to the museum gift shop. The shop was filled with people, as it always was: customers examining the scarves and neckties, the jewelry and statuettes based on the museum's most popular works. Reaching around a Texas couple who were purchasing a replica of an Egyptian cat, and avoiding a short man with a goatee examining a tie with a design of nymphs, Jon selected a woman's scarf with a pattern by Matisse to give to Lorelei.

After purchasing the scarf, he continued up the wide central staircase to the second floor and turned in the direction of the galleries that displayed European paintings. He paused briefly to make way for a covey of gesticulating Japanese, then walked on to the room that held the works of some of the Dutch masters, including Jan Vermeer.

He saw Malachi La Tour, seated on a bench in the center of the room, scribbling notations on a pad.

Jon called as he went toward him. La Tour looked up at once.

"Hey, Jonny!" La Tour stood, a brilliant smile on his face contrasting with the dark, rich smoothness of his skin. "How are you, my friend?" La Tour asked, embracing Jon. There was an easy Caribbean cadence to his voice.

"It's good to see you, Mal," Jon said.

Stepping back and studying La Tour, Jon was aware of how fit and handsome the man was. Well over six feet tall and athletically trim, La Tour was occasionally asked by those meeting him for the first time if basketball was his profession. But Malachi La Tour's passion was art history, not hoops.

In his forties, as was Jon, La Tour had an endowed professorship at Columbia, and was a popular lecturer at universities, museums, and art institutes around the world. The man's interest in art forgery was something of a sideline, Jon had learned. But La Tour had such an expert eye for spotting fakes that his services were often called upon in judging whether a work of art was what it was claimed.

"All is well with you and your family?" Jon asked.

"Couldn't be better, Jonny. Monique and the children and I hope you can visit us this summer. We've rented the same house on Georgetown Island, Maine. Do come and stay."

"I'd love to if I can," Jon said, and meant it. The La Tours were kind and gracious hosts. Jon had met them on a birding expedition to the Maine coast several years ago and seen then off and on since then.

"So what brings you to the Metropolitan today?" Jon wondered. "Real art or forgeries?"

"Both," La Tour replied. "I'm giving a lecture in Baltimore tomorrow about great artists—and great forgers—and I wanted to refresh myself on the Vermeers."

He pointed to the portrait of a woman with a lute. "Every time I look at them, I see again what a genius Vermeer was."

"And the forger is Van Meegeren, of course."

"You'll admit it's a fascinating story," La Tour said. "Although Van Meegeren lived three centuries after Vermeer, the two had lots in common. Both were Dutch, both had great technical facility, and in his own perverted way, Van Meegeren was also a genius. For a long time, even experts thought his faked Vermeers were genuine, and he profited from their mistakes."

They began walking in the direction of an adjacent gallery. "Forgery may not be the world's oldest profession," La Tour added, "but it's close."

Passing paintings by Michelangelo and Raphael, La Tour gestured up to them. "As young men, both those fellows were accused of forgery—Michelangelo, for forging a painting by his master as a student prank; and Raphael, who couldn't pay an inn bill and painted trompe l'oeil coins on a napkin so he could skip out before the innkeeper discovered he'd been stiffed."

La Tour halted at the entrance to the next room and drew Jon aside. "See those people?" he asked, nodding slightly to a group of well-dressed men and women at the far end of the gallery.

"Obviously, they're rich enough to buy the best," he said. "But I'll guarantee some of their expensive Cartier and Rolex watches are knock-offs, and they're not even aware of it. The expensive Chanel perfume several of the women think they're wearing? Nothing but cheap toilet water sold in bottles with Chanel labels pasted on. The Louis Vuitton purses? Manufactured in a sweatshop in Taiwan.

"But forgive me if I wax enthusiastic on the subject," La Tour went on. "You said you had some new forgeries to talk about. May I inquire who the real artist is supposed to be?"

"John James Audubon."

"Ah, a painter I admire greatly," La Tour said. "How much time do you have?"

"I have an early afternoon appointment," Jon told him. "After that, I'll be driving back to Scarborough."

"Then how about coming with me to my health club and after that, we have some lunch? The club is only a few blocks away. We can play a game of squash and then talk together in the steam room."

"I didn't bring sports clothes," Jon pointed out.

"I have some in the apartment that should fit you. We can stop there on the way to the club." He studied Jon. "My son is about your size. No problem."

"Yes, problem," Jon countered as they resumed walking. "Whenever you and I play squash, you beat me."

Malachi La Tour grinned. "Ah . . . but you are getting better every time. Keep at it and someday you may win."

"I doubt it," Jon answered. "And I'll need gym shoes, too."

"What size do you wear?"

"Eleven D."

"My son's size also." La Tour stopped and looked down at the loafers Jon was wearing. "They'll do nicely," he acknowledged. "But there's another question I must ask you, Jonny."

"What's that?"

"Your shoes. May I inquire where you purchased them?"

"In Rome," Jon said. "A couple years ago."

"And paid well for them, I'm sure."

"You bet. They're Ferragamo."

"True, they look like Ferragamo," La Tour told him. "But the stitching on the instep is too broad."

Jon stared at him. "You mean I was ripped off?"

La Tour laughed and placed an arm around Jon's shoulder. "I'm afraid so, Jonny. Come, let's go and play."

"YOU WERE BETTER, Jonny. Yes indeed," La Tour assured him. "One game of squash you almost won. Someday you will."

"Someday. Some year maybe, if I'm lucky," Jon said. He picked up a corner of the towel and wiped the perspiration from his face.

The two were seated on a slatted wooden platform in the steam room of La Tour's health club. Around them were a dozen or so other men, all of them naked excepted for large towels that were draped (or not draped, depending on the draper's modesty) so as to cover portions of their bodies. The heads and upper torsos of a few were hidden behind open copies of *The Wall Street Journal* and *The New York Times.*

"Now tell me more about these Audubons," La Tour said after also wiping perspiration from his face.

Jon gave him a summary, beginning with the presentation of the Audubons at Ariel McKenzie's gallery and Lasher's blistering denunciation, to Jon and Lorelei's visit to Ravener's townhouse in Boston and the man's certainty he was the suspect in Lasher's death.

La Tour leaned forward on the bench and shook his head. "You know, I'm probably one of the few people in the world—the art world, at least—who didn't hate Abel Lasher's guts. The man encouraged it, of course; he took perverse delight in being antisocial. Rumor was he deliberately shoved dirt under his fingernails every morning before going out. But I'll say this. For all his vitriol, Lasher had a discerning eye for art. And in a profession filled with phonies, he had the courage to point out those moments when the emperor was without clothes."

"He was right about the Audubon Quartet," Jon said. "At least the ones in Ravener's possession now."

"Who was the art dealer who sold the watercolors to him?" La Tour asked. "Do you know that?"

"Duncan Rutledge."

A bemused smile crossed Malachi La Tour's face. "Rutledge," he repeated. "Have you talked with Mr. Rutledge yet?"

"I'm seeing him this afternoon."

"In that case, I suggest you don't mention that you and I are friends." La Tour's eyebrows lifted playfully. "Hearing my name will only add to the man's general dyspepsia."

"What do you mean?"

"Some years ago," La Tour said, "Granby and Rutledge sold a friend of mine a small bronze statuette of the goddess

Aphrodite. Rutledge claimed it was third century B.C. My friend asked me to take a look at it. I did and something troubled me, so I researched the piece and found that the hair was wrong. If this charming little goddess came from the third century B.C., she had a hairstyle that was nineteenth century A.D. My friend asked for his money back, and Rutledge was put out, to say the least. As a dealer, he takes pride in his integrity, but in this case he should have checked the piece more fully. When I blew the whistle on the sale, Rutledge blamed me, not himself. Examining for forgeries can be a tricky business, Jonny. Take my word."

"Would you rather not look at the Audubons?"

"On the contrary, I'd like to," La Tour said. "John James Audubon and I have several things in common."

"Oh?"

"He was born in Haiti—or what's now called Haiti—as was I. And his real mother was a chambermaid like mine. Creole blood flowed through his veins, just as it does in mine."

La Tour allowed a laugh. "Of course, when he displayed his drawings to the fashionable folks of Europe, he explained his somewhat 'ruddy' skin by saying it was due to all that time spent outdoors looking at the birds."

La Tour stretched out his long legs and toweled them. "So, I will be delighted to take a look at the faux Audubons of Mr. Ravener. On Friday, I'll be traveling to Boston. I could visit his house then."

"I'll call and ask him."

"If they *are* forgeries," La Tour went on, "I'd like to show them to an expert I know at the Fogg Museum in Cambridge."

"That's fine with me. And I'm sure Ravener will be agreeable."

La Tour stood up. "I'll be at our apartment here on Thursday night. Give me a call after you talk to Ravener. If it's convenient, tell him I'll contact him directly."

"I'll do that." Jon stood also. "And thanks for your help, Mal. I appreciate it."

"Hey, Jonny—we're good friends. So let's have lunch and then I'm off to Baltimore."

"I thought your lecture was tomorrow."

"It is," La Tour said, "but an acquaintance of mine has tickets for a bird-watching event this evening."

"This evening? Not much birding's done at night," Jon said. "What birds do you expect to see?"

"Blue Jays and Orioles. Toronto and Baltimore have a night game at the stadium. Front row seats." La Tour laughed. "So I won't even have to bring binoculars."

DUNCAN RUTLEDGE SHIFTED in his chair and glowered over his half-glasses. "Granby and Rutledge has a strict policy of confidentiality concerning purchases and sales, Mr. Wilder." The small eyes did not blink. "But I am making an exception in this case because Mr. Ravener requested that I do so."

"I appreciate it," Jon replied.

"Give me several moments to refresh my memory." Rutledge opened the file that lay before him on the desk.

While the man thumbed through the sheaf of documents, Jon looked around the large office on whose walls, ironically, not a single piece of artwork hung. Rather, they were covered in a rich, wine-colored velvet, illuminated by gold sconces from which soft light glowed. Brocaded silk draperies framed a set of French doors that faced onto a terrace, beyond which the roofs of other buildings could be seen. Rutledge's office was on the topmost floor of an elegant five-story structure on the East Side of Manhattan. Once the residence of a celebrated financier of the late nineteenth century, the aura of affluence and privilege was still felt within its walls.

Duncan Rutledge himself was in his eighties, with an elongated face and bony hands with thin, attenuated fingers that reminded Jon of vultures' talons. Although the two men had never met, Jon knew Rutledge by reputation as one of the most influential and respected art dealers in the United States.

"Very well." Rutledge closed the file and looked up. "Let me add, I'll have to make this brief. As I mentioned when you called, there'll be an auction at two thirty in our auction room downstairs. I generally like to be on hand."

"Of course," Jon said.

Rutledge's long fingers steepled at his chin. "So ask me what you want. I'll answer, if I can."

"To begin, when did the Audubons first come to your attention?"

"In August of last year," Rutledge said, "we were approached by an attorney in a large Midwestern city. He informed me that he had a client, an elderly woman, whose family had owned the Audubons for many years. The woman was quite ill; she had no heirs and needed money. She contacted the attorney and asked if he could arrange a sale. He called us."

"What happened then?"

"When the man mentioned that the paintings were four undiscovered Audubons, I was skeptical, to say the least. Most works of art claiming to be previously unknown treasures almost always turn out to be fraudulent. Therefore, I insisted on inspecting them myself."

"You had them sent to you?"

"No, no." Rutledge shook his head. "If the Audubons *were* real, I didn't want to risk their being damaged during transit. Instead, we flew out to meet with the attorney and inspect the works."

"You say 'we,' " Jon said. "Do you mean yourself and Wilson Tyne?"

"Uh, yes," Rutledge responded. He took a shallow breath and then went on. "Even though he's a museum director now, Tyne knows a great deal about the works of Audubon. When we both looked at the four paintings, Tyne confirmed their authenticity."

"Why did you offer them to Ravener before anybody else?"

"Because I know he is a great collector of bird art," Rutledge said. "And because I knew he could afford the asking price."

"Which was?"

Rutledge's mouth tightened. "As I told you, Mr. Wilder, certain specifics of our business operations cannot be disclosed. Let's say it was considerable."

"Would there have been other collectors prepared to pay the same amount?"

"Indeed. Foreigners especially, for whom it would have been pocket change. But because Audubon is such a symbol of an exuberant young America, the seller wanted the paintings to remain in the United States.

"Of course," Rutledge continued, "I know all about Lasher denouncing them as fakes. The night of the Nantucket reception, Ravener called me on his way to Boston. He was furious."

"How did you respond to him?"

"I repeated my opinion that the Audubons were genuine."

The telephone on Rutledge's desk buzzed softly. "Excuse me." He picked up the receiver, listened, then hung up.

"My secretary advises me I'm wanted in the auction gallery," he said. "Do you have any further questions?"

"A few," Jon said. "Such as what may have happened to the Audubons you sold to Ravener. That is, if what he has in his possession now are fakes."

Rutledge gave Jon a sardonic glance. "If so, I suspect the present owner may be someone in The Collectors' Club. I can think of some specific names."

"What's The Collectors' Club?"

"A group of extremely wealthy individuals who have a love of art and the money to acquire it. Among them, they own many of the great works of art in private hands today. They're what you'd call the A List for every dealer in the world. I'll tell you more about them, but there isn't time at the moment. I suggest we continue our discussion later."

Rutledge gripped the arms of his chair and pushed himself up. "In the meantime, why don't you come down to the auction room? You may be interested to know that the auction features art and other objects relating to birds. As it happens, my associates have asked me to conduct the opening sale, in honor of my sixty-five years in the business." The man grunted. "On the other hand, I've had health problems recently, and they may believe this will be the last auction that I'll ever see."

He picked up a cane that leaned against the side of the desk and walked with a slow hitch in the direction of the door.

A short time later, having been guided to the auction room by Duncan Rutledge, Jon took a seat in the rear row and watched as people filed in and found chairs. At the far end of the large room, a wooden table and the auctioneer's lectern had been placed.

Jon had been given a catalogue of the auction as he entered, and he began leafing through it. Among the items being auctioned were a set of Athenian silver coins with the likenesses of owls; a large medieval tapestry depicting the phoenix and other birds out of mythology; a nineteenth-century ceremonial mask of an eagle worn by native tribes in British Columbia; and watercolors and oils done by noted bird artists, from John Gould, Audubon, and Louis Agassiz Fuertes to Roger Tory Peterson.

Several men and women gathered around the lectern and table. One woman carried a glass and a pitcher of water, which she placed on the lectern. A young man added a wooden gavel.

Scanning the room, Jon saw that it had filled. Most of those attending the auction appeared to be affluent and were smartly dressed.

But on the opposite side of the room, standing against the wall, Jon observed one man who was neither well off nor well dressed. Short and squat, he wore a blue seersucker suit. His tie was loosened at the collar; his pendulous stomach was visible above his belt. His face could not be seen behind the catalogue that he was studying; but several times, Jon saw the man's eyes glance toward him, then bury themselves in the catalogue again.

Jon watched him. Suddenly, as the man lowered the catalogue to turn a page, Jon saw his face. He wore a goatee. It was the same man Jon had seen in the gift shop of the museum earlier in the day.

The front of the room became more active. Jon noticed Duncan Rutledge approaching the lectern from a doorway. Rutledge greeted his audience, explained the nature of the auction, and announced that telephone bids would be accepted. While one assistant, a young man, stood behind him with a cellular phone, another assistant appeared at Rutledge's side and displayed for the audience's benefit a leather-bound book with illustrated parchment pages.

Rutledge pointed with his gavel to the book, announcing that the first object to be auctioned was a thirteenth-century psalter, decorated with paintings of cranes, kingfishers, wood thrushes, and other birds.

He opened the bidding at $400,000, raising it in increments of $50,000 with each bid. Initially, the bidding was noisy and brisk, but became less so when the price exceeded $1,200,000.

"Do I hear one million two hundred fifty thousand?" Rutledge called out to his audience.

No bids were offered.

"Fair warning!" Rutledge announced, looking at the crowd.

Behind him, the assistant with the cellular phone took a call. Moments later, he tapped Rutledge on the arm and handed him the phone.

Rutledge grasped it and spoke into it. Almost instantly, his face grew pale. He returned the phone to the assistant, opened his mouth soundlessly and gripped the edges of the lectern.

"Fair warning," he repeated in a voice that was barely audible. Then he collapsed.

A collective cry exploded from the audience. All stood. Rutledge's associates surrounded him, some kneeling, others calling out for help.

Jon scanned the crowd as well. What he saw was the man in the seersucker suit walking calmly toward an exit, pocketing a cell phone as he went.

6

"It's as if the Audubon Quartet is cursed," Brian Ravener said. "Abel Lasher and now Rutledge. God knows who'll be next." The heavy eyebrows lowered. He leaned back and stared out at the water. They were sitting on the stone terrace of Jon's house. Along the beach, sandpipers scurried, searching for their breakfast in the sand.

"When Rutledge and I were talking," Jon said, "he mentioned he'd had health problems, but he didn't tell me what they were."

"It was his heart," Ravener informed him. "He'd had a pacemaker installed recently. The thing apparently malfunctioned."

"But in some cases, the signal from a cellular phone can disrupt a pacemaker's impulses," Jon said. "A short time before Rutledge collapsed, he spoke with someone using his cellular phone."

"It could have been a coincidence."

"Maybe," Jon admitted. He said nothing about the man leaving the auction room soon after Rutledge collapsed.

He pointed to Ravener's empty coffee mug sitting on the table between them. "How about a refill?"

"Thanks, I'm fine," Ravener said. "And thanks, too, for letting me drop in on you this morning unannounced."

"When you arrived, you said you were on your way to New London."

"Yes. I have a manufacturing plant there." Ravener inclined his head in the direction of the driveway. "My driver's running an errand for me in Scarborough. He should be back soon. Then I'll be on my way. But before I go, I want to give you this."

He reached down beside his chair and picked up a briefcase. He opened it and took out a bound folder.

"It's the investigators' report I promised you," he said, handing it to Jon. "It's not as detailed as it might be, but I insisted that I have it ASAP. Go on. Take a look."

Jon opened the folder. What he found were several dozen pages, single spaced, as well as a covering letter addressed to Brian Ravener from Summit Investigative Services of Boston. The letter stated that the enclosed material contained the reports on the four individuals on whom Ravener had requested information. At the lower lefthand corner of the letter, the names of the four were listed alphabetically, beginning with David Bethune, followed by Jack Briscoe, Diana Cardigan, and Wilson Tyne.

"It'll give you some background on the four people I mentioned," Ravener said.

He reached into the briefcase a second time. What he withdrew now was a small white envelope. Written on the front, in elegant calligraphy, it read, 'Jonathan McNicol Wilder.' He presented it to Jon.

"What's this?" Jon asked.

"Open it. You'll see."

Jon opened the envelope. Inside was a card. 'The pleasure of your company is requested . . .' it began.

Jon smiled. "It's a wedding invitation."

Ravener smiled also. "I told Ariel I'd hand-deliver it. As you see, we've set the date for the first Saturday in August. At my Nantucket house. We very much hope you and Lorelei can be there."

"I'll ask her. It sounds wonderful."

"This time I'm going to do it right," Ravener went on. "When Meredith and I were married, it was in California in a house that was demolished by an earthquake the next year. That was an omen for our marriage, too."

"You never told me much about your first marriage," Jon said.

Ravener's face took on a look of vague regret. "Meredith and I were the wrong people for each other at the wrong time. We were both young, and ultimately we headed in opposite directions. Hers took her to Myles Coleridge. At the moment, both are probably taking great delight in my misfortune."

"Myles may be," Jon suggested, "but I don't think his wife feels the same way."

"Why do you say that?"

"Because she came to visit me the other day."

"Meredith was *here*? Why?"

"She wanted me to help you prove your innocence."

Ravener shook his head; the information seemed to confuse and baffle him. "Hard to believe," he said. "Very hard. Especially after the way our marriage ended. The truth is, I suspect Myles is playing his old tricks. I'm sure he put her up to it."

"From what I could tell, it was her own idea."

"Meredith is very good at false impressions when she wants to be," Ravener said. "In that respect, she and Myles are ideally matched."

"Well, I know you and Coleridge have been rivals."

"Rivals is hardly the word for it," corrected Ravener. "The man envies my success."

"Coleridge has been fairly successful in his own right," Jon reminded him.

"Oh, he's extremely wealthy, far more than I am," Ravener allowed. "But it's more than that. When I began collecting art, I went to auctions. Suddenly, Coleridge was showing up at the same auctions, always trying to top a bid I'd made. When I built my Nantucket house, Myles bought property on the same road and built an even bigger one . . ."

Jon heard a hesitation in the voice. "And there was the matter of my wife."

Ravener stared down at the terrace stones, marshaling his words. "When I began developing my company, I hired Meredith as my financial planner. She was resourceful and engaging and had a first-class mind. She's also quite attractive, as you know. We were together constantly; worked fourteen hour days, most weekends, went on business trips."

"And one thing led to another."

"Yes. A year later, we were married. We were also gloriously happy. That I know. But what brought Meredith and me together in the first place—the business—finally drove us apart. As it flourished, it consumed me totally. I devoted almost all my time to it; too much, as it turned out. A year and a half later, Meredith and I were attending an art auction in Chicago. Coleridge was there, too, naturally. What I didn't realize was that while he and I were outbidding one another over the items being auctioned, Coleridge had already put in his bid for Meredith. That night she announced to me he'd won. She asked for a divorce. I granted it. As soon as it was final, they were married."

"With all that," Jon asked, "why did you invite them to the reception at the Wide Wharf Gallery?"

"I didn't," Ravener responded. "Ariel did. She knew Coleridge as a collector. He'd bought several paintings from her. I'd been candid with her about Meredith, of course. But she felt it was all ancient history, and she wanted to continue on good terms with Coleridge."

The conversation was making Ravener uncomfortable. Abruptly, he stood up. "Anyway, I want to close that chapter in my life forever. Meredith is part of my past—Ariel McKenzie is my future."

The sound of a car could be heard approaching on the driveway. Ravener turned his head. "That must be my driver."

They walked toward the driveway, Jon carrying the folder and the empty mugs. As they reached it, they saw Ravener's town car pulling to a stop.

Ravener's mood was again thoughtful. "I've said it before, but I can't tell you how grateful I am for your help. After you called Duncan Rutledge to request an interview, he phoned me. He didn't want to talk with you; he said that whatever information he had about the Aububon Quartet was privileged and he didn't want to share it. In the strongest language, I convinced him otherwise."

"At the end of our interview," Jon said, "he made one tantalizing remark he never had the opportunity to explain. When I asked him who he thought might be in possession of the real Audubons, he mentioned a group called The Collectors' Club."

Ravener looked startled. "I never thought of that. He could be right."

"He said they were a group of international collectors."

"Yes. I'm one of them. And so is Coleridge. But I'm a very minor player, unlike some."

"Tell me about them."

"All are very wealthy, naturally. And all are men; they're a very chauvinistic lot. They're not an organized group by any means, and hardly a club in the official sense. They do meet once a year, though, usually at some resort or spa. I went to one of their gatherings several years ago in Baden-Baden and swore I'd never make the same mistake again. What they did most was to indulge their sybaritic pleasures in games, gambling, and women, and boast to one another about the priceless artworks they'd collected over the past year."

"Who are the major players, as you call them?" Jon asked.

"A Japanese named Takamuri. Then there's a Mexican, Ramon De Sandival. Officially, he's an investment banker, but I think his real money comes from drugs. There's also an Indonesian, an Arab sheik or two, a French count, a Dutch oil man, a German businessman, and others. This year's host is a Canadian. They're getting together in a few days in a resort north of Montreal."

"You mean their meeting is this week?"

"Yes," Ravener acknowledged. "I was invited, but declined."

An idea was forming in Jon's mind. "If I showed up at that resort on other business, say, would any of them talk with me?"

"I'm sure some would. There's nothing really secretive about the group. They're like an elite men's club, a fraternity of rich men brought together by an interest they share in art."

"Do you remember the name of the resort?"

"No. But my assistant would," Ravener said. "He handles matters of that sort. Give him a call if you decide to go."

"I will."

Ravener continued: "The more I think of it, a member of The Collectors' Club could have the real Audubons. But that's only one of several mysteries to be solved. Another is, who killed Abel Lasher?" He pointed to the folder in Jon's hands. "I still think it was someone on that list."

They reached Ravener's car. Seeing them, the driver stepped out and opened the rear door.

"One last thing," Jon said. "An art historian I know would like to have the fraudulent Audubons tested by experts at the Fogg. His name is Dr. Malachi La Tour. He'll be in Boston Friday and could pick them up."

"Fine. Have Dr. La Tour call me." Ravener gave an offhanded wave and stepped into the car. Moments later, it was gone.

Jon started to the house. He'd walked only a few steps when a raucous squawking caught his ear.

As he turned back, a huge blue jay swept past his head and landed on the top of a bird feeder that stood on a pole near the driveway turnaround. The feeder was cylindrical and had a dozen openings and perches all around for the birds.

Except that now there were no birds, because there were no seeds; that was the message the blue jay was delivering.

From a supply Jon kept in the garage, he brought some birdseed to the feeder. As he refilled it, the jay retreated to the branches of a hemlock, keeping up its noisy demands.

Returning to his house, Jon washed the mugs, then went to his study and called Brian Ravener's office in Boston. From Ravener's executive assistant he learned that The Collectors'

Club would begin its annual reunion the day after tomorrow at a place called the Golden River Resort in the town of Rivière D'Or, Quebec, north of Montreal. The gathering was planned to last three days. Jon called the resort and made a reservation for tomorrow night and the night after that.

That gave him one day to begin checking the people on the investigators' list Ravener had given him. Of the four names—David Bethune, Jack Briscoe, Diana Cardigan, and Wilson Tyne—he decided that the last on the list would be his first.

Wilson Tyne.

The reports on the remaining three listed addresses in New York City where they could be reached. He'd save them for another time. But the museum where Tyne worked was in Connecticut, albeit at the opposite corner of the state. It was a three-hour drive from Scarborough. If Jon left now, he could be there by two o'clock and home again by six.

A short time later, he guided the Range Rover onto the driveway. Glancing briefly at the feeder he had filled, he saw the blue jay had flown off, presumably well fed. In its place, a dozen smaller birds sat feasting—chickadees and titmice, goldfinches and purple finches, a bright-crimson male cardinal, even a male downy woodpecker, its red cap visible behind its head.

Living as he did, alone in a large, secluded house with few neighbors nearby, people sometimes asked Jon if he was lonely.

Not with friends like these around, he thought.

He turned the car again and started up the driveway to the road.

7

UNTIL A HUNDRED years ago, the town of New Elysium, Connecticut, was a small community of farmers and farm families, as well as tradespeople on whom the agrarian economy depended—the blacksmith, the provisioner of feed and grain, the grocer, and the dry-goods merchant. When the community was settled around 1800, it was known commonly as Swillville, for the number of pig farms in the area.

Then in the 1950s, real estate developers bought many of the farms, built large, expensive homes and succeeded in convincing city dwellers that a better life was to be had there, far from urban ills. Soon, superhighways put the town within driving distance of New York and Hartford. Others found its rustic charms ideal for a weekend getaway. Almost overnight, the town adopted a veneer of style and sophistication; the two remaining farmhouses that had not fallen to the wreckers were declared historic structures by the state. The town's name was changed to New Elysium, suggesting the place in Greek mythology wherein the blessed dwelled. (The fact that the blessed dwelt there only after death was never mentioned.) Main Street kept its name, but lesser roads like Old Sow Way, Misery Lane, and Muddy Gully Street did not. Bassett's Candy and Ice Cream Emporium was bought by an investment group and the name changed to Le Palais de Glacée et Chocolat. The clock repairman now advertised himself as a horologist.

Still, as Jon drove through the town, he noticed it retained a resolute New England character that time and recent residents with different values and priorities could not destroy. He found the Simon Kreutzer Museum at the south end of Main Street among homes built in the Greek-revival style.

The white-painted building itself was of neo-classical design, set well back from the road. Its simple elegance was in sharp contrast to the large, abstract works of sculpture, many of them metal, that had been placed around the grounds.

Jon parked in the staff section of the parking lot, as Wilson Tyne had suggested he do when Jon called. To his surprise, he saw Tyne coming down the walk in his direction.

"Very punctual," Tyne said as Jon stepped from his car. "It's two exactly."

Wilson Tyne was someone who obviously prized punctuality. In his dark suit, white shirt, and striped, regimental tie, he seemed the model of an English bank clerk, the image aided further by an immense forehead and the aquiline nose on which rimless glasses sat.

"A pleasure to have you visit the museum," Tyne said. "Let's take a walk. I'll show you some of the new acquisitions in the sculpture garden."

Jon agreed.

The two men walked through an arbor and emerged in a grassy area among which were set the stone and metal sculptures Jon had noticed earlier. They included a giant stabile by Calder and a reclining nude in stone by Henry Moore. There were also lesser works by lesser artists, one of which appeared to be the jagged remnants of a Chevy Nova transformed not by the imagination of its sculptor, but by a particularly nasty demolition derby.

As they passed it, Tyne gave it a disparaging glance. "That piece is called 'Order Out of Chaos.' Personally, it's not my taste," he said, "but Mr. Kreutzer liked it, so he purchased it."

Tyne indicated a stone bench beside the walk. "It's getting warmer. Shall we sit and rest a bit?"

Jon nodded and both sat down on the bench. "And how would you describe your tastes?" Jon asked.

"More traditional. In particular, I admire the American Realist painters of the nineteenth century."

"Such as Audubon?"

Tyne looked at him. "Yes, such as Audubon." He paused. "I gather Ravener has told you it was I who authenticated the Audubon Quartet."

"Yes. Duncan Rutledge also mentioned it."

"Then let me repeat unequivocally, the Audubons we saw were genuine. I know a great deal about Audubon's technique. There's no question he was the artist of the watercolors we were shown."

"Did you spend any time with them alone?"

"Why? Do you think I photographed them or made notes and sketches of them to be later forged? The fact is, I detest forgeries of any sort."

"Then you think the Audubons unveiled at the gallery *were* forgeries?" Jon asked.

"I have no idea. I wasn't close enough to study them."

"But Abel Lasher was convinced they were."

"It was Abel Lasher's nature to destroy," Tyne said. "Whether it was a painting's reputation or a person's, it was all the same to him."

"How well did you know Lasher?"

"You ask the question as if you already know the answer."

"I know some things, yes," Jon said.

"May I ask you what things in particular?"

"I know that you and Lasher talked about something at the reception and that you seemed very upset."

Tyne shifted on the bench and looked up at the sky, which had begun to fill with clouds. Either he was attempting to refresh his memory, or was confronting something in it that was deeply troubling.

"I also know," continued Jon, recalling what he'd read in the investigators' report, "that for the past several years, large checks were drawn on the museum to pay for ads in Lasher's magazine."

"That's true," Tyne said. "I wrote the checks myself. They paid for advertisements for museum exhibitions."

"Except that the amounts were double the magazine's usual ad rate. Why was that? Was Lasher pocketing the extra money?"

Wilson Tyne sighed heavily. "Since you know, others obviously do too. It was bound to come out anyway. When I was a young gallery assistant in SoHo, the owner of the gallery invited several of us for a weekend at his house in the Hamptons. The last night we were there, he had a party. The party—how shall I put it?—eventually got out of hand. Everyone had had too much to drink; the pot was plentiful. At some point, people began taking off their clothes—and began doing things that later they would very much regret."

Pain showed in the man's eyes, but he went on. "Several

years ago, when Simon Kreutzer was considering me for the directorship of this museum, Lasher called me. He told me he was in possession of some photographs that had been taken of me at that party; photographs, he said, that Mr. Kreutzer would consider 'shockingly depraved,' and that would cost me any chance of getting the museum job. Lasher said he was sure he and I could work out an arrangement whereby we could keep the photographs a secret."

"In other words, Lasher was blackmailing you."

"Yes."

"How long did it go on?"

"I was still paying him," Tyne admitted. "He approached me again at the reception about a payment that was overdue. We had words; I was quite angry. But I didn't kill him. I may have wanted to a thousand times. But murder takes a certain kind of courage, and by nature, I am not a courageous man."

They were interrupted by the arrival of a U-Haul rental truck. It swung into the parking lot and stopped beyond Jon's car. The driver's door opened and Jack Briscoe jumped down from the cab. As he caught sight of Jon and Tyne sitting on the bench, he waved. The two men stood. What's Briscoe doing here? Jon asked himself.

Tyne must have read his thoughts. "I've been expecting him," he said. "Mr. Kreutzer bought a painting of Briscoe's earlier this month. Briscoe said he would deliver it today."

Briscoe loped across the parking lot, giving them a jaunty grin as he approached. "Hello, Wilson," he announced. "And look who's here as well—Jon Wilder, the birds' best friend. Cheerio, Jon. We meet again."

"How are you, Jack?"

Except for the dark glasses, Briscoe was dressed like a working artist—paint-smeared sweatshirt, ragged denim shorts, and hiking boots that also bore spatterings of paint. He shook Tyne's hand, then Jon's.

"Sorry I'm a bit late, Wilson," Briscoe said in his affected British accent, "but I had to make a petrol stop."

"You have the painting, I assume," Tyne said.

"It's in the U-Haul with some others," Briscoe said, nodding toward the truck. "It's quite large, though. I'll need a lad to help me carry it."

"I'll get one of the assistants," Tyne responded. He glanced over at Jon. "I may be a while. Would you care to wait?"

"No. I'll be going," Jon said. "Thanks for your time."

There was the distant sound of thunder. The three looked up simultaneously at the rapidly darkening skies.

"I hate to say it," Briscoe observed, "but I think we better get the painting in before it rains."

Tyne excused himself and headed back along the walk to the museum.

"Congratulations on your sale to the museum," Jon told Briscoe after Tyne had gone.

"Thank you." Briscoe sounded pleased. "Kreutzer himself saw it at a one-man show of mine at a TriBeCa gallery and bought it on the spot. Generally, I loathe having to make nice at gallery shows." He chuckled to himself. "I'd much rather spend time in a back booth at McGivney's Pub hoisting a pint. Anyway— Aren't you a bit out of your turf, Jon?"

"How so?"

"Artistically, I mean. Have you abandoned drawing pretty birds in favor of abstract art?" He grinned. "Don't get me wrong. I like birds, too. Preferably in their twenties. There were some lovely ones at that Nantucket reception, wouldn't you agree?"

"I'm afraid that's not what most people will remember about that night," Jon said.

"You mean the nasty row between Ravener and Lasher? Doesn't surprise me in the slightest if Ravener killed him when he had the opportunity."

"Is that what you think happened?" Jon asked.

Briscoe gave a shrug of non-concern. "Well, someone did. And none too soon. The world's a better, safer place now that Lasher's spending his eternity in critic's hell."

"I gather you didn't like the man."

"Not much. He savaged me in my last show, you know. But, of course, he referred to Pablo Picasso as 'the dago doodler,' so I'm in good company, at least."

Footsteps sounded on the walk. Jon and Briscoe turned to see a muscular young man coming toward them. "Mr. Tyne sent me," he announced as he arrived.

"The painting's in the U-Haul," Briscoe told him. "Come with me." He started to the parking lot, the young man at his heels.

Jon watched them. Arriving at the truck, Briscoe opened the rear doors, then jumped up on the loading gate and disappeared inside. Soon one end of the painting was visible as it rolled out on a dolly. The painting was extremely large and covered with gray packing quilts.

While the young man stood below, Briscoe swung the dolly lengthwise, pulled away the quilts and threw them back inside the truck. Uncovered, the abstract painting measured about fourteen feet by six. Briscoe lowered the gate, holding the painting at one end. Once within his reach, the young man took the other end and together they began carrying it up the walk to the museum.

Studying the abstract from a distance, Jon thought it recalled the early works of Jackson Pollack. But this painting lacked the spontaneity and zest that Pollock showed. In contrast, Briscoe's work, as colorful as it appeared, was tame.

Briscoe was a skillful craftsman, that was obvious. But whatever gods embrace certain artists with the gifts of inspiration, passion, and originality, they had given Briscoe only a passing nod.

Jon started for his car. As he passed the rental truck, whose rear doors had been left ajar, he stopped and looked inside. He saw what he assumed were other paintings secured against the walls. All were smaller than the abstract, but covered with the same gray quilts. Except for one. Its quilt had fallen to the floor. Studying the painting, Jon saw that it was a seascape with a single sailboat, her billowing white sail set against dark clouds and a churning sea.

Jon heard a noise from the direction of the parking lot. He looked back to see Jack Briscoe running toward the truck.

"Forgot the papers," Briscoe said as he arrived. "Can't get paid without the paperwork."

He went to the driver's door of the cab, opened it and grabbed an envelope lying on the floor. He stuffed it in a pocket of his shorts, then started back to the museum. As he passed Jon again, he noticed the open rear doors of the truck.

He glanced at Jon uncertainly. "I seem to have forgotten several things." He stepped up to the doors, closed them and secured the lock.

"Hope to see you again, Jon," he called as he hurried back across the lot.

You will, Jon thought.

Something was wrong.

Jon knew it the moment he pulled into the driveway turnaround beside the house and stopped the car.

The return from New Elysium had been swift and uneventful. He had escaped the rain, and for the most part there was little traffic on the roads. The dashboard clock of the Range Rover had blinked to 6:13 P.M. as he arrived. He'd pressed the automatic door control on the sun visor, and the garage door had just begun to lumber upward when the feeling came to him.

Something was wrong.

Jon stepped out of the car. He scanned the house and the surrounding woods. Everything about the house seemed just as he remembered when he'd left for New Elysium. The woods, as always, appeared dense and dark and undisturbed. Looking past the house in the direction of the water, the scene was placid.

What was different now?

It was the silence.

Except for the faint lapping of the waves against the shore and the distant cries of gulls, there was no sound.

His eyes went to the bird feeder he had filled that morning. Not a single bird perched at the feeding holes. In the bushes near it, no birds sat.

Then, slowly, Jon looked down to the area of dirt in which the feeder had been placed. The birds were there—the crimson cardinal, goldfinches, chickadees, titmice, the woodpecker with the bright red cap.

Now all were dead.

"SO—WHO KILLED Cock Robin?" Lieutenant Lawrence Leydecker knelt at the base of the feeder, studying the tiny corpses of the birds.

He raised his head to face Jon. "But I guess none of these is a robin, is it?"

"No."

"Weird. Very weird." The lieutenant's face became more saturnine than usual. "I've been with the Scarborough Police thirty years, and this is the first case of mass birdicide I've seen."

He picked up a plastic bag and a set of pincers lying on the ground. "You said the birds were dead when you got home?"

"Yes. That's when I called you."

"Okay. I'll bag 'em as evidence. And the birdseed, too." One by one, Lydecker began picking up the dead birds with the pincers and dropping them in the plastic bag.

"What will happen to them now?" Jon asked.

"I'll send them to the state's forensic lab for testing," Lydecker said. "The medical examiner is used to getting human stiffs. Let's see what he can do with birds."

For the dour police officer Jon had always considered Lydecker, the man displayed great tenderness in handling the birds. Finally he lifted the last of them—a brightly colored male goldfinch—and inspected it closely. The bill was open and there was evidence of blood inside the mouth, as if the bird had hemorrhaged internally. Otherwise, there were no marks of violence.

"I think they were poisoned," Jon volunteered. "Probably by a very toxic pesticide added to the seeds."

Lydecker gave a concurring grunt. "Little buggers didn't

even have a chance to fly away. Just ate the seed and dropped." He looked at Jon. "Did you put anything different in the feeder when you filled it?"

"The usual mixture," Jon said. "Nothing that I hadn't used before."

"And you said you left the house about eleven?"

"Yes. I filled the feeder just before I did."

The lieutenant stood up and leaned close to the bird feeder, studying the seeds that still remained inside. "It looks to me," he observed, "like somebody came visiting while you were gone."

"I guess," Jon told him, wishing he could ignore the thought.

"Can the feeder be detached from the pole?" Lydecker asked.

"Yes."

"Good. I'll take it with the seeds inside." Lydecker scrutinized the lid. "And whoever did this probably removed the lid. So maybe there are prints."

"I should have an empty cardboard box in the garage for you to carry it in," Jon said. He started toward the turnaround.

"And bring a trowel," Lydecker called after him. "I want a sample of the loose seeds on the ground."

Jon continued into the garage and found an unused carton that was small enough to hold the feeder upright. From a rack that held small tools used for gardening, he took a trowel.

As he returned, the lieutenant was opening a second plastic bag. Taking the trowel, Lydecker began scooping up the loose seed that had fallen from the feeder and dumped it into the bag.

Jon knelt opposite him. "When will you know what sort of poisoning agent was used?"

"Soon, I hope." Lydecker continued scooping. "I have a friend with the state police toxicology lab. I'll give him a call."

Lydecker lifted the plastic bag and pondered it. Satisfied with what he'd gathered of the loose seeds and soil, he rose. "How do you detach the feeder?" he asked.

"Lift it off the pole from below."

Gingerly, Lydecker separated the cylinder from the pole that supported it and placed it in the box.

"What will you do now?" Jon asked, walking with Lydecker as the man carried the box and plastic bags to the patrol car. "I mean, about finding out who did this?"

"First, I'll speak to your neighbors," Lydecker said. "How many houses are there besides yours on Plover Point? Three?"

"Yes. I'm the last, and fairly isolated, as you know."

"As I know," Lydecker repeated, frowning. "I'll also speak to the folks on the main road. Maybe someone saw a stranger in the area."

"Will you tell them what happened?"

"What? That some unknown person came while you were gone and poisoned your birds?" He shook his head. "They'd worry their own pets would be next."

Lydecker opened the passenger door of the police cruiser and placed the box and plastic bags on the front seat. "I'll tell them," he continued, "that there've been reports of break-ins around town. No more than that."

He waved a hand in the direction of the house. "I mean, you're fairly isolated here, to quote you. Make that *very* isolated, Jon. Your driveway is long and winding and overgrown with trees. Your nearest neighbor is at least three hundred yards away.

You've got woods on this side of the house, and a beach in front connected to a nature sanctuary. Someone could walk along the beach without anybody spotting him. If he surprised you—and if he meant to do you harm—nobody would know."

"Larry, if you weren't a friend, I'd almost think you're trying to make me paranoid."

"Face it, Jon. You choose to live here by yourself."

"That's also comforting."

"Anyway," Lydecker went on, "I'll plan to step up patrols in the area. My guess is that whoever did this won't be back. He's probably some screwball who hates birds and wanted you to know the way he felt. When he didn't find you home, he killed them."

"Instead of me?"

The lieutenant frowned again, but didn't answer.

"I wasn't going to mention this," Jon said, "but I have a suspicion somebody has been following me."

"You're right. You are paranoid. Who's following you, Jon? And why?"

"Who it is, I don't know. As for why, probably because I'm doing sort of an investigation."

"*Sort* of an investigation? What's that supposed to mean?"

Briefly, Jon gave him the background: the matter of the Audubons, Abel Lasher's murder, and Ravener's request for help. Lydecker listened without comment, but his look of skepticism did not fade.

"Recently when I was in New York," Jon went on, "I saw this little man in the gift shop of the Metropolitan Museum. Later that day, I saw him again at an art auction."

Lydecker shrugged. "Could be a coincidence."

"I doubt it. I also have a feeling he's the one who killed the birds."

"Why would he do that?"

"To warn me to back off. To forget the Audubons. To stop asking questions about Lasher."

"So what's he look like, this stalker of yours?" Lydecker took a notepad and pen from his shirt pocket.

"Average height, fortyish, white, and somewhat overweight. With a goatee."

"Except for the goatee, he sounds like half the male population of America." Lydecker finished scrawling the information on the pad. "But if I see him on the streets of Scarborough, I'll let you know."

"You won't. He has a city look about him."

"City look? What's a 'city look'?"

"Savvy. Streetwise."

"Not your simple country constable like me." Lydecker achieved one of his infrequent smiles.

He returned the pen and notepad to his pocket and started for the driver's side of the police car. Jon joined him. Lydecker opened the door, then turned to Jon.

"Keep in touch," he said. "And let me know if anything out of the ordinary happens."

"Such as?"

"Strange phone calls. Letters in the mail. And don't open any packages if you don't know who the sender is. If you have any questions, punch in nine-one-one and ask for me. I'll make sure you get through."

"Thanks, Larry."

"By the way," Lydecker said, "what's your schedule for the week ahead?"

"I thought I'd fly up to Canada tomorrow," Jon answered.

"What for? To do some fishing?"

"You could call it that."

"How long will you be gone?"

"A couple of days at least."

"So the house'll be empty. Nobody around."

Jon nodded. "Nobody."

"Then I'll have one of our officers drive down to check things once a day when he's on road patrol."

"I'd appreciate that, too. Thanks."

"Just make sure your alarm system is working."

"I will."

"And one more thing." Lydecker looked back in the direction of the house. "I notice you have other bird feeders. Take them down. Put 'em inside the garage or somewhere. But get 'em out of sight. Whoever killed the birds probably won't show up again, but if he could do a thing like that once, who knows what he's planning next?"

Lieutenant Lydecker climbed into the police cruiser and closed the door. The engine sprang to life. "See you, Jon. Take care."

He paused, looking up at Jon through the open window of the patrol car. "Take care," Lydecker said again.

8

After flying for an hour over forests of evergreens that seemed to go on endlessly, Jon decided that the symbol on the flag of Canada should be the pine cone, spruce bough, or hemlock sprig rather than the maple leaf.

He'd taken an early flight from Providence to Montreal, cleared Customs, and gone directly to a complex of buildings bordering the airport. Among them were the offices and hangars of a fleet of smaller aircraft that ferried guests and visitors to resorts some distance from the city. Jon went to the plane scheduled to fly to the town of Rivière D'Or, where the Golden River Resort was located, and joined the twenty other people heading there as well. Once airborne, the plane quickly left Montreal behind and flew north toward the Laurentian Highlands.

From his seat near the rear, Jon studied his fellow passengers. Among them were seven couples, most of whom appeared to be Americans. The remainder were men of varying nationalities. A few carried slender leather cases, which Jon guessed contained disassembled fly rods.

Abruptly, the airplane decreased its speed. Looking down, Jon saw they were descending. He could make out beyond a ridge below what appeared to be a tiny airstrip at the base of a long valley. Less than a minute later, the plane dropped onto the strip with a teeth-jarring thump, slowed with sudden force, and taxied toward a low log building that was the airport terminal. Along one wall was a sign announcing *"Bienvenue à Rivière D'Or, Quebec."* Beneath it was the same greeting in English: "Welcome to Golden River, Quebec." Jon also noticed a number of small private aircraft parked along the far side of the runway. Some of the members of The Collectors' Club, he guessed, had already arrived.

He deplaned, feeling the cool, dry air the moment he stepped to the tarmac. Carrying a light suitcase, along with a camera and binoculars, he walked through the small terminal building to the entranceway beyond. He saw several large white vans directly opposite. The words "Golden River Resort" were emblazoned on their sides.

As he and a few others moved toward the vans, with Jon bringing up the rear, a young man stopped him. "Excuse, monsieur—but because of extra luggage, there is no more room. Please to take a taxi, if you would."

Glancing at the vans, Jon didn't see a problem over space. But by now, an old black Chrysler Imperial was making its way across the parking area in his direction.

"The taxi driver is in the pay of the resort," the young man explained, gesturing to the Imperial. "So there will be no charge to you."

Jon decided it would be easier to acquiesce, so he agreed.

"Très bon," the young man said. He opened a rear door of the car. At the same moment, the driver, a dour French–

Canadian with a taut, leathery face, stepped out, walked back to the trunk and opened it. The young man took Jon's case and put it in the trunk. The taxi driver slammed the trunk lid, lit a Gaulois, and slipped in again behind the steering wheel.

"Enjoy your visit to Golden River," the young man said and began to close Jon's door.

Before he could, another man's hand grasped the handle and held the door open.

"Arrêtez! Wait!" a voice said. The man to whom the hand belonged leaned down. "Mind if I join you?" he asked Jon. The face was darkly handsome, with broad cheekbones and Hispanic features.

"Not at all," Jon said. He slid over on the seat to give him room. The driver turned his head and scowled silently at both of them.

"Thanks," the man said, settling into the back. "The seat I was given on the van was next to a woman who was perfumed like a musk ox." He extended a hand to Jon. "Please let me introduce myself. I'm Ramon De Sandival."

"Jon Wilder." He shook the man's hand. At the same time, Jon guessed that this was the Mexican investor and possible drug lord Brian Ravener had mentioned.

Meanwhile, the taxi had pulled out behind the vans and was making its way along the exit road, away from the airport terminal.

De Sandival made himself comfortable and took a long, deep breath. "Ah—the air of the Canadian woods. Such a difference from what I left behind. In Mexico City yesterday, you couldn't see the buildings for the smog."

"Is Mexico City your home?" Jon asked.

"Yes, and Cuernavaca. I have a residence in each place, as

well as a house overlooking Acapulco Bay. And you are an American, of course. What brings you here? A vacation?"

"My profession, really," Jon said. "I'm a painter of birds. Just north of the town of Rivière D'Or there's a wonderful nature preserve. I thought I'd visit it later this afternoon."

It was the story Jon had planned to use to publicly explain his visit. The prime purpose, of course, was to meet the men who made up The Collectors' Club and learn what he could from them. But the proximity of the preserve to Golden River had been ideal. A short drive from the resort lay one of the most interesting, if not the largest, nature preserve in Quebec Province. Throughout its densely wooded mountains were numerous varieties of plants and animals, including birds. Jon's only other visit had been years ago, and he was glad he had a reason to return.

Ahead, the vans turned onto a two-lane highway, and the taxi followed. Almost at once, the vehicles slowed and moved to the right, relinquishing a good part of the road. Jon realized the reason for their caution: coming toward them at high speed was a massive, fully loaded logging truck. Passing them, the air and backwash rocked the taxi, shoving it onto the shoulder of the road. Cursing, the driver wrenched the wheel with both hands and returned the car to the road.

"So what can you tell me about this resort, the Golden River?" De Sandival asked. "It's my first visit."

"Mine also," Jon said. "To the resort, I mean. I've been to the preserve before, but I didn't stay at the resort."

"Maybe the driver can tell us something about it." De Sandival leaned forward and tapped the man on the shoulder. "Excuse me," he said, "but can you give us some information on the Golden River Resort?"

Either the driver was deaf or he deliberately ignored the question. Instead, he gripped the wheel tighter and continued staring straight ahead.

De Sandival was not deterred. He tapped the driver's shoulder for a second time. "Pardon, monsieur," he said in a louder voice. *"Parlez vous Anglais?"*

"*Non.*" The driver tossed his Gaulois out the window and spat after it.

De Sandival leaned back in the seat and sighed. "Damn French Separatists. The man's probably spoken English all his life, and now pretends he can't." He turned his attention to the passing scenery.

A short time later, the vehicles slowed again and swung into the entrance of the resort. With its great gate of stockade logs and twin gatehouse, also made of logs, Jon had the impression they were approaching some sort of well-armed and well-provisioned fort, fully able to defend itself against the outside world. Their arrival at the large octagonal building that was the central lodge reinforced that feeling. What it defended, Jon decided, was the privileged way of life its wealthy guests enjoyed here, protected from the cares of those less fortunate who lived beyond its walls. Given the money that obviously flowed into it, the resort was aptly named.

Jon checked in at the front desk, went briefly to his room, then returned to the café restaurant off the lobby and had a late lunch. Leaving the lodge, he began a stroll of the grounds. He had passed the tennis courts when from beyond a wall of tall privet hedges, he heard men's voices, occasionally interrupted by the *thock* of mallets striking wood.

He located a path among the hedges and turned onto it. What he discovered was a beautifully manicured croquet court.

A row of benches bordered the area on the near side. Several men were seated on the benches, while others stood holding croquet mallets. They were dressed in leisure wear, except for a tall gentleman in a dashiki. All were watching the game that was in progress. Even from where Jon stood, the internationality of the group, players and spectators both, was evident. He could see several Asians; a small man with a mustache who appeared to be Middle Eastern; a blond gentleman, possibly a Dutchman; and an Arab, undoubtedly from a ruling family, in a loose-fitting white abas.

Jon walked toward the benches nearest him. As he did, the man seated at the end turned. It was De Sandival.

"Ah—Mr. Wilder," he called. "Please come and join us. Are you a player of croquet, by any chance?"

"I'm afraid not," Jon said. He sat down beside De Sandival.

"Neither are most of my colleagues," De Sandival said, chuckling. "They prefer more gratifying indoor sports like gambling and women. But our Canadian host has put up a substantial purse to the man who achieves the winning score, and few could resist."

Jon saw a Japanese man coming toward them, as did De Sandival, who waved. "Toshi . . . come and meet a newfound friend of mine, Jon Wilder. Jon, this is Mr. Takamuri."

Mr. Takamuri stopped before them, bowed and beamed. "Most pleased to make your acquaintance, Mr. Wilder. Are you a recent member of our group?"

"What group is that?" Jon asked him, ingenuously.

"Mr. Wilder is an artist," De Sandival explained. "A painter of birds."

"Indeed, indeed," Takamuri said. He beamed again and sat

down. "We Japanese are very fond of birds. Particularly cranes and doves. My last acquisition was a set of paper screens painted in the Edo period—a display of doves."

"Many of our friends enjoy bird art as it relates to their own country," De Sandival said. He pointed to the Middle Eastern man, who was measuring the distance to a croquet wicket in anticipation of his shot. "Dr. Pyandi is Iranian, and as a former member of the Shah's inner circle, he loves peacocks. Hans Rogmans, our Dutch friend, is fond of storks. As for my fellow Mexicans, our flag depicts the eagle as it kills a snake."

He half turned to Jon. "But an eagle also appears on every American dollar bill. What did your great bird artist, John James Audubon, call the eagle?—'the noblest bird that has yet been discovered in the United States.' "

"You're obviously familiar with the works of Audubon," Jon suggested. He waited for De Sandival's response.

"I am," De Sandival allowed. "I've also followed with interest the purchase of four undiscovered Audubons by a man with whom I have done business—Brian Ravener."

"How was it you did business with him?" It was something Ravener hadn't mentioned.

"Last year Ravener wanted to set up a factory in Tijuana," De Sandival said. "He approached a number of investors. I was one of them."

Takamuri spoke up: "However, I have heard that the Audubons Mr. Ravener possesses now are forgeries, and that he himself might hold the key."

"What do you mean?" Jon asked.

"He insured the paintings for a great amount of money," Takamuri explained. "If it is proved that the four originals were stolen, or in some way disappeared, then Mr. Ravener would benefit from an insurance settlement." He added, "I have heard he is in need financially."

"Considerable need," De Sandival agreed. "The business of the Tijuana factory confirmed it. After the investors gave him money to construct the plant, something went wrong. The deal fell apart, and Ravener was thrust deeply into debt. An insurance settlement over those presumably missing Audubons would go a long way in covering that debt."

"What do you mean 'presumably missing'?" Jon inquired.

The Mexican regarded him. "There's also speculation that Ravener himself stole the originals, arranged for fake ones to be substituted, and hid the real ones where they could not be found."

From the croquet court, someone called De Sandival's name. Looking out, they saw the Dutchman beckoning in the direction of the bench.

De Sandival stood up and took his mallet. "Excuse me, but it's my turn to rejoin the game." He looked at Jon again. "Do you have any plans for dinner, Mr. Wilder?"

"No. None at all."

"Good. Then perhaps you would be free to join me and several of my friends, among them, Mr. Takamuri."

"Indeed, indeed." Mr. Takamuri nodded enthusiastically.

"I'd like that," Jon said. "Thank you."

"The resort has set aside a private room for us," De Sandival went on. "Do you still plan to visit the nature preserve this afternoon?"

"For a short while, yes."

"Then let's say dinner about eight. I'll leave a message in your room with the details."

"That would be fine," Jon told him. "I look forward to it."

"So do I," De Sandival said. He gave the croquet mallet a quick spin, caught the handle in midair, and proceeded toward the court.

As HE CAME down the front steps of the lodge, the first thing Jon saw was the Chrysler Imperial parked directly opposite. The same driver was leaning nonchalantly against a fender smoking a cigarette, the same sullen expression on his face. Jon guessed he was probably a local from the town, who had no other work and hung around the resort hoping to cadge business from the guests.

Jon walked toward the car, carrying his camera and binoculars. "Pardon, monsieur. The Lac aux Fauçons nature preserve. Do you know it?"

The man gave a slight nod. "Oui, monsieur. I can drive you there."

"How long a trip is it?"

"Peut-être—perhaps a half hour, monsieur. You said you wished to see it."

Jon recalled mentioning to De Sandival during their airport ride that he hoped to visit the preserve that afternoon. "Yes, that's true. I do," Jon said. "But I won't stay long. Maybe just about an hour, and then we can head back here."

"Oui, monsieur." The man reached over and opened the rear door of the car. Jon climbed into the back seat.

"Bon," the driver said. He climbed into the Imperial and headed down the entranceway of the resort toward the main road.

They drove in silence for some miles. As they did, the terrain became increasingly rugged, the car's engine struggling and gasping as it pulled up the steep inclines.

"Beautiful country," Jon observed to the driver.

The man lit a cigarette and shrugged.

"Are you from around here?" Jon continued. "Do you live in Rivière D'Or?"

"Non."

So much for the driver being local, Jon thought. He abandoned any thought of further conversation and returned to studying the scenery. He could see a pair of golden eagles soaring above a ridge line on broad wings. Once in the preserve itself, Jon knew he would see many more, as well as hawks and harriers, and the falcons for which the major lake of the preserve was named.

Then something drew his attention back to the interior of the car: it was the driver's right hand making adjustments to the rearview mirror. At least the man was concentrating on the road, Jon thought. And just as well. Mammoth logging trucks, large as railroad cars and traveling as fast, continued to pass them, some coming from the opposite direction, others sweeping around them from behind with an intimidating roar.

When the man grasped the mirror for a second time, Jon looked around, expecting to see a logging truck gaining on them from the rear. To his surprise, the only vehicle he saw was a dark blue Oldsmobile a hundred yards behind, traveling at the same speed as the Chrysler.

Jon looked at his watch. It was four-fifty. Although sunset would not occur till after eight, the road was already half in shadow, cast by the steeply wooded slopes to each side. Then, without even looking back, Jon realized the car that had been following them had turned on its headlights.

A sign flashed by along the gravel shoulder of the road: *"Lac aux Fauçons—4 km."*

Jon moved over on the seat and leaned forward behind the driver. "I seem to remember that the entrance to the preserve is on the right. There'll be more signs as we get closer to it."

The man did not respond. Instead, the car began to slow. Jon guessed the man misunderstood what he had just said.

"I meant, the entrance is a couple of miles yet," he said. "We've got a ways to—"

The next instant, the car skidded to a near stop; Jon was slammed against the seat back. The car spun left, then accelerated up a rutted dirt road that rose sharply among trees.

Finally, it stopped. The driver flung open the door and began running, half-stumbling, through the dust to the main road.

Jon leaped out also and was about to shout after the still-running figure, when he saw the other car. The blue Oldsmobile had pulled into view along the side of the main road and stopped. A rear door opened as the taxi driver reached it and jumped inside.

Watching it, Jon expected the Oldsmobile to race off. It didn't. Instead, it made a swift U-turn and stopped again. The window on the front passenger side lowered and a face appeared. Sunglasses covered the eyes, but beneath the chin, the man had a goatee. Then Jon saw something else. At the base of the open window, the man's hands were clenched around a pistol. It was pointed straight at Jon.

A bullet shattered the Chrysler's windshield on the driver's side. Glass flying around him, Jon dove for cover in a stand of small pines along the side of the dirt road.

The second shot followed almost immediately, ricochetting off a boulder near where Jay lay and embedding itself with a soft thump in the trunk of a hemlock to his right. The third slammed into the car again: Jon heard the impact of metal penetrating metal and prayed it hadn't been the gasoline tank that was struck.

Heart pounding, he pressed his face against the fallen branches and pine needles of the forest floor, wondering desperately what part of his body would take the next bullet. It never came. He felt a sudden moment of panic, guessing the shooter had gotten out of the Oldsmobile and was walking up the dirt road toward him to make certain that the final bullet found its mark. What Jon heard instead was the squeal of tires against asphalt.

He lay there for several minutes waiting, listening, before he raised his head. From around a fungus-covered tree stump, he saw the opening through which the main road was visible. The road was empty. There was no sign of the Olds.

Slowly, Jon stood up and looked around. The Chrysler sat squarely in the center of the dirt road. A slight wind had come up; he was aware of the trees rustling above him. It was the only sound he heard.

Then, distantly, he heard another. At first it was so indistinct and subtle that he couldn't make it out. It was a low but steady rumble, interrupted by a fitful, angry hissing sound. When he'd jumped from the car, he'd wondered if this rough separation in the trees had been a firebreak. Now he knew it was a logging road. The rumble, growing louder every moment, was that of a logging truck making its way down the steep decline to the main road: the hissing sound, the air brakes slowing the truck's momentum as it approached the twisting curves.

Jon felt the earth begin to shake under his feet; the rumble had become a constant thunderclap. Turning toward its source, he saw that fifty yards from where he stood, the road curved sharply left among thick pines. Then, through the pines, suddenly he saw it—the chrome grille, the high cab section, the first set of the truck's gigantic wheels; and finally, the truck itself, its topmost logs snapping away low, overhanging branches as it came.

Instinctively, Jon bolted for the trees, away from the road. He caught his foot on ground vines, kicked through them, staggered forward and fell, rolling into a grove of pines.

The logging truck, seeing the car directly in its path, blasted its horn. Brakes locked, the truck skidded, swerved to one side and back again, smashing the left half of the Chrysler from front to rear while mowing down a swath of new-growth trees at the side of the road. Throwing up a cloud of dirt and stones, the behemoth skidded the rest of the way down to the main road, swung onto it, and came to a wrenching, screeching stop out of Jon's sight.

Jon heard a voice shouting in French and the sound of running footsteps. He started out of the grove of trees in the direction of the logging road. Passing the Chrysler, he knew that if a driver or passenger had been on the left side of the car, he would have been killed when the truck hit it. Looking down into the wreck, he saw his camera and binoculars lying on the floor of the back, lenses shattered, the camera split and useless, the film spiraling out.

"*Imbécile!* Idiot!"

Jon glanced toward the main road again to see a tall, fully bearded man approaching him, waving his arms and bellowing French curses as he came. Jon knew it was the driver of the truck. Between the expletives the driver flung at him, he also knew the man believed the car was Jon's.

Jon raised a hand. "I will explain," he called in shaky French, and started down the logging road.

9

THE RITZ CARLTON Hotel in Montreal was not where Jon had planned to spend the night. But he was glad to be alive to spend it anywhere. After making his predicament apparent to the driver of the logging truck, the man had driven him into Rivière D'Or. At the local police headquarters, Jon gave a statement detailing what had occurred from the time he was picked up at the resort by the man driving the Imperial to his encounter with the logging truck.

After returning to the lodge, he'd found the manager profuse in his apologies. The so-called taxi driver had had no connection whatsoever with the resort, the manager assured him, nor did the fellow at the airport, who had steered Jon to the car. As a gesture of goodwill, the man offered Jon free lodging for the remainder of his stay, an offer Jon declined. Instead, he asked to be returned to Montreal, as well as for overnight accommodations there, if they could be secured. The manager had acquiesced.

It was now nine-thirty in the morning. Jon sat in the hotel restaurant, consuming a croissant and listening to the men at the next table volubly debating the Expos' chances of capturing a division title the next year. His return flight to Providence was scheduled to depart at noon. He still had time to pack and get to Dorval Airport without hurrying.

He was about to add marmalade to the croissant, when he saw the maitre d' approaching him.

"Pardon, Monsieur Wilder," the man said, "but I believe you have a call." He handed Jon a telephone.

"Jon! Thank God, you're all right!" Ravener exclaimed the moment Jon was on the phone. "I placed a call to you at the resort last night. They told me what had happened, and where you could be reached in Montreal. But I decided to wait until this morning. I also called the provincial police and the police in Rivière D'Or. They didn't want to talk. Have you learned anything more?"

"A few things, yes," Jon said. "The Chrysler, or what's left of it, was checked for fingerprints. It seems the driver was a paroled car thief by the name of Luc Pinchon. As for the man with the goatee who shot at me, they have no leads."

"I'm sorry, Jon. I mean that honestly. You're a good friend, and I can't tell you how much I appreciate everything you've done. But I want to keep you *and* our friendship alive for a long time. So if you want to call it quits, I'll understand."

"Thanks for giving me the out," Jon answered. "But right now I'm angry. Also, I'm more sure than ever that I want to see this through. Yesterday somebody tried to kill me, and I'm damn well going to find who he is and why he wants me dead."

"Even so—"

"I mean it," Jon informed him. "As soon as I get back, I'm going to New York to talk to the other people on that list."

"All right," Ravener acknowledged finally. "But I'll repeat

what I said earlier; if there's something, anything, that I can do, just tell me."

"As a matter of fact, there is a detail that you've never mentioned. Was the Audubon Quartet insured?"

"Of course. But if you're asking whether I filed an insurance claim, the answer's no. I've had a few business setbacks lately when the money would've come in handy, but I can get it in other ways." He added, "And the truth is, I still expect the real Audubons to be returned."

"I DON'T LIKE it," Lorelei insisted, and began dusting some Imari china in the display window of her shop. Jon sat on a stool, watching her.

"Don't worry. I'll be fine."

"How can you say that after what happened in Canada? You were very lucky, Jon."

"I know that."

"And now you're telling me you're going to New York?"

"Lieutenant Lydecker still plans to have the Scarborough police check the house while I'm away."

"It's not your house that I'm concerned about. It's *you,* your safety. And your life."

"I'll be careful."

"Will you be home tonight?"

He shook his head. "I have a talk to give before a birding group tomorrow evening. I'll be back the morning after that."

Lorelei set down the dust cloth and faced him. "Don't go. Please."

He took her hands and held them gently. "Don't worry," he repeated.

"I can't help it."

"I'm not a first-time tourist to the city, you know. Years ago I lived in Greenwich Village."

"Twenty years ago, to be exact. And you were a student then."

"I'll be fine."

This time she didn't answer but shot him a look that said, "I am not angry with you, stubborn and wrongheaded as you are," and returned to dusting the Imari. The truth was, Jon had never seen her visibly angry about anything. Instead, her eyes would narrow and her voice would take on a high, thin quality that she herself admitted made her sound like Minnie Mouse.

"Listen, I'll call you later from the Stanhope," he assured her. "After my lecture tomorrow night, I'll also call. The morning after that, I'll drive directly back to Scarborough."

"Promise?"

"I promise." He stepped down from the stool and started for the door. He turned and added as an afterthought, "The next two days will probably be remarkably uneventful."

"I'd like to believe that," Lorelei said.

So would I, Jon thought.

UNTIL RECENTLY, A section of the West Forties of Manhattan had been called "Hell's Kitchen," and on this summer afternoon it more than lived up to its name. As Jon walked past the brick tenements and brownstones, he decided that the temperature was stuck on "Broil," with no hope of relief in sight.

Before he left Scarborough, he had telephoned the three people on the list he hoped to see: Jack Briscoe, Diana Cardigan, and David Bethune. Jack Briscoe had been unreachable, both at his apartment and at his studio in Greenwich Village. Diana Cardigan had said she would see Jon in her office at *Au Courant* at three. When he'd spoken with Bethune, the man had been initially reluctant, but agreed to meet with Jon at two at the loft building where he lived and worked.

Bethune's address turned out to be a stolid gray-stone building, metal-clad, that had probably once been a turn-of-the-century sweatshop where newly arrived immigrants toiled long days under execrable circumstances for a meager wage. Today, as Jon approached, he saw a trio of young men sitting on a row of trash cans; for them, work seemed the last thing on their minds. Colt 45 cans in their hands, they moved in rhythm to the grunge rock blaring from the boom box at their feet.

Jon entered the building, found Bethune's name among the list of occupants, and pushed the button. A moment later, the loudspeaker crackled.

"Yes?" the filtered voice asked. It was Bethune.

"David, it's Jon Wilder."

"Oh, yes. When I buzz open the door, walk through to the elevator and take it up to the third floor. I'll meet you there."

A buzzer sounded. Jon pushed open the inner door and walked a short distance to a large elevator, covered only by a sliding metal gate. After a considerable pause in which the ancient cage seemed to be deciding whether to operate or not, it slowly rose.

As it approached the floor, Jon saw first the feet, then the complete form of David Bethune, dressed only in sandals and blue jeans. Bethune reached to slide open the elevator gate. As he did, Jon noticed that a large bandage covered the back of Bethune's left hand.

"Sorry for the informality," Bethune said, indicating his limited attire. "In the summer, this is the way I usually work."

He led Jon to a door and opened it. Jon moved into the loft after him. The space was vast, and stiflingly hot in spite of the efforts of an air conditioner that could be heard wheezing like an asthmatic in an adjoining room. Along one wall a set of windows rose twenty feet or more.

But it was what occupied the other walls that drew Jon's attention most. The walls were covered with exquisitely painted portraits of nude women. All of them appeared to be young, in their late teens or early twenties.

When Jon turned back to Bethune, he found the artist studying him with a bemused expression. "You're curiosity is obvious. And understandable. I prefer the company of men, of course. But it's women who are the subject of my art. I find the female form the most glorious of natural creations. And if I do say so myself, I paint them very well."

Bethune moved to a small table and picked up a bottle of Evian water. He unscrewed the cap and held the bottle out toward Jon. "Care for some? I'll get a glass. It's very good on a hot day."

"No, thanks."

Bethune took a sip from the bottle and then raised it aloft. "Some people say it defeats the purpose of drinking bottled water if it's stored in plastic. Impurities get in. But I have bad luck with glass bottles. Somehow I'm always breaking them and getting cut."

"Is that what happened to your hand?"

Bethune regarded him before he spoke. "No. Actually, I did this on Nantucket. The night of the reception, Wilson Tyne and I were walking to the ferry dock; I slipped on the wet cobblestones and fell. My hand hit the stone curb."

He waved Jon to a settee, then sat on a high stool opposite him, balancing the bottle on one knee.

"Excuse me if I can't spend the time in lengthy chitchat. But this is a very busy day. I have an opening in a few days at a gallery on Wooster Street—the Scorpio Gallery—and there are several paintings still to finish. I have a model coming soon to pose for one of them. So I'd appreciate it if we could make our visit brief."

"Of course."

"By the way, I saw some of your bird paintings at the reception. They were very good. Wilson thought so, too. Ravener had invited him, and I came as Wilson's guest." He added, "Wilson and I are friends."

"At the reception, did you also have a chance to look at the Audubons that Ravener displayed?"

"Yes. I was standing near them at the front."

"And do you believe they were forgeries, as Lasher claimed?"

"I have no idea. I'll confess I dislike birds. I have a phobia about them; I've been terrified of them since I was a child."

"On the matter of forgeries, are you familiar with the techniques a forger uses?"

The limpid blue eyes studied Jon. "You've heard the story, then," Bethune said. "It's not really a secret. On the other hand, it's not something I feature on my resume. I've always had a special talent as a copyist; that is, reproducing skillfully the works of other artists. One day a collector of some reputation called and ask me if I'd make a copy of a Modigliani painting that he owned. Why he wanted it, he didn't say. As it turned out, the collector took the copy I'd made and tried to sell it as the real thing. When it was discovered to be bogus, the collector put the blame on me; he said I knew about the swindle and had demanded a percentage of the sale price."

"But the charges against you were withdrawn, I understand."

"Yes. While the matter was being investigated, the collector died. Without his testimony, the officials dropped the case."

"Is that why Lasher always referred to you as 'the artist/forger' when he reviewed your work?"

"I'm sure," Bethune answered. "And, of course, he always savaged everything I've done. But I had another reason for disliking the man."

"Oh?"

"You're an artist, so you know how important public exposure is when you're trying to develop a career. What I didn't know when I was younger were the rules of the game. How the professional art world functions when there's money and reputation to be made. Some years ago, I was to have a one-man show, my first, at a prestigious uptown gallery. Suddenly, with no explanation, I was told that another artist had been substituted in my place."

"Because of Abel Lasher?"

"Yes. I learned the other artist was a young man whose career Lasher wanted to promote. The young man also happened to be a nephew of the benefactor who put up the money to start Lasher's magazine."

Bethune leaned forward on the stool. "I'll say this and I mean it. I'm not sorry the man's dead."

From the adjacent room, a telephone began to ring. Bethune excused himself and went to answer it. Against the wheezing of the air conditioner, the conversation was inaudible. But Bethune's voice rose above it briefly. The words "I need you this afternoon" and "I'll have it" could be heard.

Waiting for Bethune's return, Jon made a slow circuit of the room. To one side of the room was a large easel. On the easel he saw what was probably Bethune's current project: an oil painting of a nude young woman reclining on a chaise. Beyond the easel was the chaise itself. Presumably, the model who occupied it in the painting was the one the artist was expecting.

Next to the easel was a table on which Bethune had placed his paints. There was a broad range of colors, many in the soft flesh tones.

There were also several small jars neatly labeled as to their contents.

One jar held gold metallic paint.

"Pick your poison," Diana Cardigan said. "Are you here to talk about Abel Lasher's murder or Brian Ravener's fake Audubons?"

She took a deep draw on her cigarette, flicking away the fallen ashes from the blue caftan she wore.

"Then you think the Audubons were fakes?" Jon asked.

She gave him a brief smile. "If Lasher said they were, they had to be. He was the expert."

"Did you get a look at them at the reception?"

"Not a good look, no. After the brouhaha between Ravener and Lasher, Pesky and I left the gallery."

"But you'd seen the Audubons before then," Jon said. "Ravener had shown them to you a month earlier at his house."

She confirmed it. "Yes, that's where I first saw them. Or rather, Pesky and I did. I'd heard through the grapevine that

Ravener had come into possession of the paintings, so I called him and proposed doing a piece on them in *Au Courant.* He was sympathetic and invited me to his house to see them. What he showed me at the time looked genuine."

She opened a desk drawer, searched through it with both hands, then slammed it shut with a loud "Damn!"

She looked desperately at Jon. "You're not a smoker, are you?"

"No."

"Damn," she said again. "I figured not."

She stood up. "But I may have a pack left in the files. I sometimes hide them in the file cabinet when I'm trying to give up smoking. Let me look."

She eased sideways around the desk and went to a metal file unit that stood against the wall. She pulled out the top drawer and rummaged through it, closed it and continued downward, searching through each drawer without success.

As she did, Jon took the opportunity to look around. The office appeared miniscule; hardly suitable, it seemed, for the feature editor of a popular arts magazine. It was also spectacularly disarrayed. The surface of the desk itself was covered to a depth of several inches with newspapers and magazines, as well as with what appeared to be a racing form, a half-eaten bagel smeared with peanut butter, several crumpled pages from a yellow legal pad, and a metal ashtray, mounded with spent cigarettes and so enormous it could have functioned as the hubcap of a truck.

"Gotcha!" Diana Cardigan cried out. She reached into the bottom drawer, pulled out a pack of cigarettes and proceeded to rip open the top. As she returned to her desk, she saw that Jon was studying the room.

"I know the office is a mess. But that's a statement of fact, not an apology." She lit a cigarette. "Another fact is, I'm a slob. Ironic, isn't it, considering the image that the magazine projects. Refinement . . . Culture . . . Elegance. And here I am sitting in this office no bigger than a brothel cubicle, up to my ears in crap."

She relit her cigarette, which had gone out. "Now, let's talk about the recently departed Mr. Lasher. Before we start, you ought to know that I'm not the one who murdered him."

"Do you have any idea who might be?"

"Probably Brian Ravener. It makes sense, doesn't it, after the way little Abel publicly denounced the Audubons?"

"How well do you know Brian Ravener?"

The woman thought and shrugged. "Not well. I met him first when he was married to the dragon lady."

"Meredith?"

"The very one. The present trophy wife of Myles Coleridge."

"It sounds like you're not fond of her," Jon offered.

"Quite the contrary. She has the beauty and the grooming of a show cat. And the claws to match. But maybe I'm just envious. Most women would be. Men adore her, and she's relentless when it comes to getting her own way . . . as she invariably does."

"Then do you think she could have murdered Lasher?"

"She may have had a motive."

"What do you mean?"

"Two years ago, Lasher did a piece in *Art Now* about wealthy collectors. 'Fine arts philistines,' he called them. And he named Myles Coleridge in particular. I met the Coleridges at a reception soon after the article came out and I asked them what they thought of it. Coleridge laughed it off, but Meredith was furious; she said somebody should step on Lasher for the insect that he was."

She waved the cigarette in Jon's direction like a wand. "Now let me ask you a question. Who was it who sicced the p.i.'s on me? I can't prove it, but I know somebody's been poking into the sinkholes of my life."

"It wasn't me."

"Then it was Ravener. That figures. If I was trying to beat a murder rap, I'd do the same. So what's the story, Jon? Did Ravener hand over their report and ask you to follow up?"

"Brian Ravener's a friend," Jon said, "and I agreed to help him prove he's innocent. I think he is."

"Then you already know lots about me, from the brand of Scotch I'm fond of to the names of my bed partners. Am I right?"

"Well . . ."

"I withdraw the question. I'm embarrassing you." She laughed, leaning forward on her elbows, fingers intertwined. "I like you, Jon. So I'll confirm something you probably already know. Abel Lasher was preparing an attack on *Au Courant.* And on me . . ." She paused. "I'll also tell you something you *don't* know . . . only a few people do. Abel Lasher was one. But now he's dead, so that's one less."

She pulled the ashtray over and crushed out the cigarette, breaking it. "Abel Lasher was my husband," she said.

"I beg your pardon?"

Diana Cardigan lit another cigarette and leaned back in her chair, amused. "Frankly, I expected more of a reaction from you, Jon."

"I'm surprised, I'll say that."

Her amusement lingered. "Don't worry. I'll spare you the

macabre details. They'd make headlines in a supermarket tabloid look tame. Mercifully, most of our unholy matrimony was a blur, thanks to alcohol and controlled substances that I consumed in an uncontrolled way."

She held out her left hand and spread the fingers. "You'll notice I'm not wearing a wedding ring. Abel bought a ring on the condition that I pay for it. I never did."

"How long ago was this?" Jon inquired.

"Thirty-seven years. Time flies." For a brief moment, there seemed a look of wistful melancholy on her face.

"He and I were art students at Cooper Union," she continued. "One night a group of us got drunk. It was around midnight; Abel and I had been exchanging personal attacks the way we always did. Then out of the blue, somebody bet that if the two of us were married, the marriage wouldn't last two days. Everyone loved the idea—except for Abel and myself, of course. But together, the others in the group raised over a hundred dollars. Much as Abel and I loathed one another, we were in desperate need of money, so we took the bet. The bunch of us piled into cars and drove to some place in Maryland that was a marriage mill. We found a justice of the peace, woke him up, and got him to perform the ceremony in his bathrobe. At three-thirty in the morning, Abel Lasher and I became man and wife."

She blew a quantity of smoke in the direction of the ceiling, watching as it rose. "It was in June. My mother always thought I'd make a wonderful June bride."

She looked at Jon again. "After the wedding, we drove back to Manhattan and picked up where we'd left off, the boozing and the joints. Dawn came. The other students stumbled homeward. And the bride and groom began their married life together sleeping in a drunken stupor on the floor. We woke up about noon and started screaming at each other, just the way we had the night before. Which one of us came up with the absurd idea we should consummate our marriage, I don't know. But the attempt was a disaster. Hideous. Bizarre. I finally stormed out, went to the apartment of a friend and slept till the next day. At three-thirty that afternoon, the newlyweds agreed to call the whole thing off."

"You got a divorce?"

"Not officially, no. But the other students felt so sorry for us, they gave us the money they'd put up for the bet. Naturally, Abel kept it for himself, the bastard."

"But you were still legally married to him when he died," Jon said.

"I suppose so. For whatever it's worth."

"It might be worth something if he left a will. There are his assets. His holdings on the magazine, the proceeds—"

"If he had a will," she interrupted, "I'm quite sure I'm not the beneficiary."

"Does he have any heirs you know of? Any family?"

"No." She shook her head. "At least, I never heard him mention them. His parents died when he was seven, and he was brought up by his grandmother. Personally, I think the man was sui generis; I'd hate to think of others in the family with his genes."

The office door abruptly swung aside and Pesky Swift appeared. He was wearing a T-shirt that said "Photographers Do It With an F-Stop."

"Hi, Di," Swift called in. "Got those contact sheets on the Cellinis on the layout board. You want a look?"

He noticed Jon and waved. "Yo, Jon—I didn't see you."

Jon stood. "Hi, Pesky." He turned back to Diana Cardigan.

"You've got business to take care of, so I'll be off. Thanks for your time."

"I'm always pleased to see you, Jon," she told him. "Although I won't say it was a pleasure talking about Abel Lasher. It never is. Call me if you need anything more."

"I'll do that."

Jon retreated to the hall. He was about to close the door, when he discovered Pesky Swift had followed him.

"Hey, like, I wonder if you could do me a favor," Pesky said as he caught up with Jon.

"What's that?"

"There's these photographs of birds I took," continued Swift. "Since you're a bird expert, maybe you could take a look at 'em."

"Well . . ."

"I can send them to your house. No rush. I'd really, you know, value your opinion."

"Okay," Jon relented. "Let me give you my address." He found a pen and notebook in his jacket pocket and wrote out the address.

Swift took it and read it. "Great. I'll get 'em in the mail in the morning. You should have 'em in a day or so."

"That's fine," Jon said. He started down the hall.

LEAVING THE OFFICES of *Au Courant,* Jon headed east in the direction of Times Square. He had turned the corner at Ninth Avenue when he began to pass a photographic-supplies store. Seeing it reminded him of certain items that he needed for his work.

He entered the store and went to the counter that sold camera carriers. He explained to the clerk that he was looking for a leather shoulder strap that could be hooked onto a camera bag in order to replace the strap he'd lost. Of the several models the clerk showed him, Jon chose a strap of sturdy dark-brown cowhide with metal clasps at both ends for attaching to the bag.

He bought the strap. The clerk placed it and the receipt in a plastic bag and Jon started from the store. As he approached the door, he noticed the section that sold optical equipment. He attracted the attention of the young woman behind the counter, who had just concluded a sale of binoculars.

"Excuse me," Jon said to her, "but I'm looking for a spotting scope. A small one."

He gave the make and model number and told her that it was smaller than most scopes currently in use. On certain birding trips, he'd found the spotting scope to be more portable and useful for his purposes than binoculars.

The young woman made an inspection of the display case without success. "Let me check the stockroom," she said and headed toward the rear of the store.

While Jon waited for her to return, he gazed idly through the store's front windows to Ninth Avenue. Traffic on the avenue was heavy, but the heat and torpor of the summer afternoon seemed to have reduced pedestrians to a scant few.

"You're in luck," the sales clerk announced as she returned. "We have one left."

She placed it on the counter. To the observer, the scope had the appearance of a tiny telescope: a black cylinder about four inches long, less than an inch wide at the larger end and even smaller at the other, where the viewer's eye was placed.

Jon purchased the spotting scope and put it in the plastic bag with the camera strap. When he stepped out onto the sidewalk again, he walked to the curb, peering up the avenue for a taxi that would take him back to the hotel.

It was at that moment that Jon noticed him.

The man was across the street, directly opposite from where Jon stood. The figure turned his back to look in a shop window.

Jon thought at first it was his imagination playing tricks.

But as he continued staring at the man, he knew what he'd seen was true . . .

The man had a goatee.

10

JON BEGAN WALKING south along the avenue, now and then glancing into the store windows beside him. In their reflection, he could see that the man was moving also, always a short distance behind, but casting furtive looks in Jon's direction as he walked.

Abruptly, Jon halted and pretended to scan items in the window of a hardware store. Across the street, the man stopped also, as if jerked suddenly on puppet strings. With his back to Jon, he appeared to be studying the merchandise of a shop selling ladies' lingerie.

Jon turned the corner, heading east in the direction of Eighth Avenue. Ahead, on his side of the street, he saw the marquee of a motion picture theater that specialized in film revivals. The current offering, he noticed, was Alfred Hitchcock's 1963 classic of suspense *The Birds*.

Appropriate, Jon thought, for what he had in mind.

At the ticket window, he bought a ticket for himself. Looking over his shoulder as he entered the theater, he noticed that the man had crossed the street to the same side as the theater and was flipping through the contents of a newsstand magazine rack.

Pocketing the ticket stub, Jon crossed the lobby and slipped into the theater. The feature was well underway. On the screen, the young blonde heroine was hurrying along a country road in a convertible, a look of worry and impatience on her face.

Jon moved into the rear row at the left side of the theater but remained standing, letting his eyes grow accustomed to the diminished light. As they adjusted, he observed that the audience was small and concentrated mostly in the center toward the front.

He moved farther into the row and sat down beside the wall where it was darkest.

Less than a minute later, as Jon knew it would, the door to the lobby opened. In the shaft of light that streaked through momentarily, he saw that the newest moviegoer was the man with the goatee. The door swung closed and all was dark again.

As Jon had done, the man stood in the aisle, letting his eyes adjust. Then, unexpectedly, he took a step backward, standing in the aisle beside the row where Jon sat.

To Jon's relief, the man moved forward finally and took a seat some rows ahead in the center section of the theater.

Glancing at the screen, Jon saw that the heroine was now seated on a bench next to a large, white, one-room schoolhouse. Behind her were the school playground, the swings, jungle gym, and seesaws. From inside the schoolhouse, the voices of singing children could be heard.

Jon knew the film was approaching a climactic scene. If the man wanted to kill him, this theater would be the place for it.

And soon, when noise, screams, and pandemonium would be erupting from the screen.

Jon wouldn't give the man that chance.

Looking at him again, Jon saw that he remained standing in the middle of the row he had entered, peering at the members of the audience in front of him. At last, the man lowered himself into a seat.

Jon rose, slipped out into the aisle and made his way forward, touching the seat backs as he moved. To his relief, the row in which he planned to sit was empty. He edged along it as quietly as possible until he was directly behind the man. He folded down the seat and lowered himself onto it.

Aware of someone at his back, the man stirred but kept his attention focused on the screen.

From the plastic bag, Jon took the camera strap. He tied one end of it into an adjustable loop that could be tightened if the strap was pulled. Next, he withdrew the spotting scope and in the dark, used his fingers to determine which was the smaller end.

In a swift gesture, he slipped the looped part of the strap down over the man's head and pulled it taut around his neck.

The man gasped. Both hands flew to the strap.

"Don't call out," Jon whispered at his ear. "And don't move."

With his other hand, he pressed the small end of the spotting scope against the back of the man's head.

The man pitched forward in his seat.

"I said, don't move."

He jerked the man upright with the strap and jammed the scope harder against his head.

The man sat rigid.

"Good. Now let me ask you, do you know what's pointed at your head?

A convulsive swallow followed. The man's hands clutched at the strap.

"Since you're having trouble answering," Jon hissed, "maybe it'll help if I describe it. It's black. Steel. About four inches long. And I am very good at using it. Do you know what it is?"

"A gun."

Jon didn't bother to correct him.

"So now that we've finally met," Jon said, "I'm going to ask you a few questions. What's your name?"

"Eddie."

"Eddie what?"

"Stagg."

"Stag, like the deer?"

"With two g's."

"Well, Eddie two-g Stagg, unless you want your head to be a trophy on my wall, tell me why you're following me."

Ahead, on the screen, the heroine was growing visibly uneasy. In the playground behind her, a single crow had flown down and alighted on the jungle gym.

"Why are you following me?" Jon repeated.

"I'm not."

"Truth, Eddie, truth. Your memory's short. I'll refresh it. The museum gift shop. The art auction. Did you call Duncan Rutledge on a cell phone just before he died?"

Silence.

Jon twisted the strap tighter, keeping the scope against Stagg's head. "Did you?"

"I didn't know he was gonna die."

"Why did you call him?"

"To tell him not to talk to you."

"Why not?"

"You were trying to know too much about the pictures."

"The pictures? You mean the Audubons?"

"Yeah, them."

"Is that also why you followed me to Canada? And why you shot at me? Because I was trying to find out more about the Audubons?"

"Yeah."

"Who hired you to do that?"

In the dark, Jon could hear Stagg struggle for a breath.

"Come on, Eddie. None of that was your idea. Who hired you to follow me? *Who?*"

Heads turned in the audience, and hushing sounds could be heard.

"Who?" Jon said again, softly.

"Coleridge."

Jon was startled. "Myles Coleridge?"

"Yeah."

Stagg continued to stare forward. On the screen, the heroine had lit a cigarette, still unaware that in the playground behind her more and more huge crows were sweeping down and landing on the jungle gym.

Jon raised the spotting scope and pressed it firmly into the fatty flesh on a direct angle with the cortex of Stagg's brain.

"Let me tell you something, Eddie," he said. "Trying to kill me is one thing. But when you killed my birds, you made me very, very angry. Was that your own idea, or was that also 'orders'? *Answer me.*"

At once, there was loud shushing from the audience.

Jon removed the spotting scope, but kept the strap still

cinched around Stagg's neck. He quickly tied the other end of the strap to the bottom of Stagg's chair, where the metal frame was bolted to the floor. Any effort on Stagg's part to rise would tighten the loop around his neck.

On the screen, the heroine turned back, suddenly terrified to see that the jungle gym was filled with crows.

Jon leaned forward and whispered in Stagg's ear: "I'm going to go now and have a word with your employer. But don't get up on my account. In fact, I wouldn't recommend it. Stay and watch the movie."

He added: "The best part's still to come. The birds get their revenge."

JON CLOSED THE heavy book and tossed it on the bed.

Returning to the Stanhope, he'd gone immediately to his room and searched for the name of Myles Coleridge in the Manhattan telephone directory. He'd found two Coleridges, neither with the name of Myles. Among the business listings, there was a Coleridge Typesetters on Coenties Slip, and a Coleridge Meat Purveyors on Gansevoort Street.

Jon was disappointed but not surprised. Myles Coleridge was a very private man. He had a duplex on the East Side of Manhattan and an estate somewhere north of New York City, as well as the house that overlooked Nantucket Harbor. But there were no listed phone numbers at any of them. He controlled a variety of businesses, but none that bore his name.

The bedside clock showed 5:15 P.M. Jon debated what he should do next. Brian Ravener would probably know how Coleridge could be reached. But if Jon called him, Ravener would start asking questions for which Jon didn't have the answers. Yet.

He finally decided on an early dinner in the hotel. Afterward he would come back to the room and spend the evening studying his notes for the lecture he would give before the birding group tomorrow night.

First, though, he would allow himself a short, pre-dinner nap. He lay down on the bed and closed his eyes.

The ringing of the telephone woke him almost at once. He rolled to his side and grabbed up the receiver, mumbling "Hello."

"Jon?"

The voice jarred him awake. "Lorelei?"

"Are you all right?"

"Fine. Tired is all. Where are you calling from? The shop or home?"

"I'm in the lobby."

"Of the hotel?" He sat up on the edge of the bed. "What's wrong?"

"Nothing's wrong. Except I've been worried about you since this morning."

"I'm fine. Really."

"You don't sound fine. You sound strange."

"I've had a strange day," he admitted. "What are you doing in New York?"

"I'll explain when I see you. I can see you, can't I?"

"Certainly. Come on up." He gave her the floor and number of the room.

"I'll be there in two minutes."

It was two minutes exactly when Lorelei stepped into the

foyer of Jon's suite. He closed the door and followed her into the large room that overlooked Fifth Avenue.

"How about something to drink?" He unlocked the self-serve bar.

"Maybe just a soda." She flopped down in a chair. "Summer is icumen into New York and I'm parched."

He poured a diet soda over ice and brought it to her, then pulled up a chair. "Now tell me what you're doing in the city. Besides being worried about me, I mean."

"There's an antiques dealer on Second Avenue who was offering old Waterford crystal for a song. So I drove down this afternoon and bought the lot."

"And you're driving back tonight?"

"Tomorrow."

"You mean—"

She stopped him with a smile. "Sorry. I'd prefer a lovely stay-over at the Stanhope, but I promised friends who have an apartment on East Eightieth I'd stay with them. They've been asking me to visit them for months."

"But—" she went on brightly, "it turns out that my friends have to attend some sort of charity event and I can't see them until later . . . so I went ahead and made dinner reservations for us at seven at Café des Artistes."

"Sounds wonderful."

Lorelei checked her watch. "Even so, that still gives us an hour."

"That also sounds wonderful," Jon said.

Again, the telephone rang. Jon frowned and picked it up.

"Jon—" Myles Coleridge greeted him pleasantly. "I do believe a talk between us is in order."

"It's 'in order,' all right," Jon said grimly.

Lorelei looked puzzled. Jon mouthed Coleridge's name.

"I'm calling from my home in Dutchess County," Coleridge went on. "I suggest you join me for dinner."

"When? Tonight?"

"Tonight."

"Sorry, Myles," Jon informed him, "but I have other plans."

"Forgive me," Coleridge added, "but the invitation also includes Mrs. Merriwell."

"How did you—"

"With the city still so hot, I'm sure you'll both find a visit to The Aerie quite refreshing. That's the name of my estate, you know," Coleridge explained. "It's high and overlooks the Hudson River. In the summer, there's a lovely evening breeze. We can have drinks on the terrace first."

"I told you," Jon said, "I have other plans."

"Then break them." It was a command.

"Jon," Coleridge continued, "you are a person I admire greatly, both as an artist and as a man. I also know you're a close friend of Brian Ravener, and because you are, you're trying to help him out of his present fix. Am I correct about that, Jon?"

You arrogant bastard, Jon thought. "Yes, you're correct," he said.

"To that end," Coleridge told him, "there are certain questions that you seek the answers to, which only I can provide. Would you pass up an opportunity to have those answers? You would not.

"Therefore, you and Mrs. Merriwell will join me for dinner at The Aerie. My driver will pick you up at the hotel in fifteen minutes. Please be prompt."

11

IT WAS CONSIDERED one of the great houses of America, in the same class and with the same distinguished pedigree as mansions of the Vanderbilts, the Rockefellers, and William Randolph Hearst's San Simeon. But unlike them, The Aerie, which Coleridge had acquired fifteen years earlier, remained a place in which not a single tourist had set foot. Or ever would, by all accounts, if Coleridge had his way. There were rumors he had instructed that upon his death, the house was to be leveled and the rubble pushed over the cliff into the Hudson River, above which it grandly sat.

The house and grounds occupied over a thousand acres that included several lakes, a vineyard, a variety of gardens, as well as tennis courts, a riding stable, and a firing range accommodating armaments of every kind. At one corner of the property there was also a landing strip and a hangar in which Coleridge kept his private multiengine plane: a Piper Navajo.

The house itself was a vast Tudor-style structure built of granite, brick, and oak timbers, with a roof of blue and gray slates, and provided a complete panoramic view of its surroundings. To the east could be seen the foothills of the Berkshire Mountains; to the north and south, the verdant woodlands of the Hudson Valley, dotted with other and smaller estates. To the west, and far below, the Hudson River shimmered in the summer twilight like a ribbon of bright sequins. Beyond, and stretching westward, were the Catskills, ridge after ridge undulating in a chiaroscuro pattern before disappearing into the evening haze.

"Nice pad," Lorelei remarked as the limousine bearing her and Jon swept past the wrought-iron gates and started up the winding sycamore-lined drive.

As the car slowed before the house, Jon glanced through the side window. He was surprised to see Myles Coleridge himself, hands on his hips, standing at the top of the entrance steps that led up to a set of massive doors. The man was dressed in a loose-fitting white shirt, white breeches, and black boots. Given a whip, Jon decided, Coleridge could double as a lion tamer. The man's outfit, plus his look of absolute control, would be enough to dominate the beasts.

On the other hand, Jon wondered if he was putting his head in the lion's mouth, as well as jeopardizing Lorelei, by coming here. But when he'd told her of Coleridge's invitation, she'd urged him to accept and wouldn't let him go alone. She'd also reminded him of what Coleridge had said: that only he could provide certain answers that Jon sought.

The limousine had barely glided to a stop when the chauffeur leaped out and opened the door on Lorelei's side, then raced around and opened Jon's.

At the same time, Myles Coleridge began to saunter down the steps, his face and head a smooth, almost cherubic, pink.

"Lorelei, Jon," he called. "Welcome to The Aerie."

Approaching Lorelei, he grasped her shoulders and gave her a firm kiss on the lips. He turned to Jon and took his hand. "I trust the trip was satisfactory for you both."

Jon nodded. "Fine."

Coleridge turned to Lorelei again. "And what a pleasure that you could join us. The presence of a lovely woman such as you enhances any gathering."

"Will your wife be here, too?" Lorelei asked pointedly.

"Unfortunately, no. Because of the heat, Meredith chose to return to our Nantucket house. I thought of flying there myself this afternoon." He cast a fleeting look at Jon. "But business—and other matters—made it advisable that I remain here."

Coleridge gave them an ingratiating smile. "As I said earlier, I thought we would have cocktails on the terrace. There's a path that leads down through the garden. Follow me."

He turned and started off along a walk. Lorelei and Jon moved quickly to keep up with him. Soon the pathway wound through a meticulously tended garden, full of summer flowers, and arrived finally at a broad stone terrace. At the far end of the terrace was a large swimming pool, occupying several levels, with cascading waterfalls between. Beyond it was a low, white-stucco building that Jon guessed was a pool house.

Coleridge guided them to a set of teakwood furniture, grouped around a glass-topped table. Two large Italian market umbrellas, both of them white, overspread the furniture and table.

"Please make yourselves comfortable," Coleridge instructed them. After Jon and Lorelei chose chairs, he stretched out on a chaise lounge. "If either of you cares to take a swim, you'll find the pool very pleasant."

Jon and Lorelei declined.

"Very well then. Let's have drinks." Coleridge raised a hand. As if anticipating his master's signal, a young servant suddenly appeared, dressed in a white shirt and black trousers. The boy was in his teens, with features that were almost femininely delicate.

"Cocktails, Angel, *por favor,"* Coleridge said to him.

The young man bowed, then turned to Lorelei and Jon. Each requested wine.

"The usual. Vermouth cassis," said Coleridge before the servant scuttled off across the terrace.

"Angel is the newest member of my serving staff," Coleridge explained. "He hates it when I call him Angel. He would prefer I use the Spanish pronunciation of 'Ahn-*hel.'* "

Coleridge locked his hands behind his head and stretched out along the chaise. "Now, wasn't I right? Isn't it much cooler here than in the city?"

"It's beautiful," Lorelei assured him. "And so quiet."

"The railroad line runs directly below, along the riverbank," Coleridge said. "Now and then I hear the train. In the evening, the engineer of the Montreal express loves to blow the horn. But I don't mind. It reminds me of my childhood."

"Where was that?" Jon asked.

"Kentucky," Coleridge said.

Lorelei reacted with surprise. "Kentucky? Really? You don't have any trace of an accent."

Coleridge's gray eyes regarded her. "My father was a white sharecropper. I've made it a point to lose traces of everything concerning those years of my life."

The servant returned with three Baccarat crystal wineglasses on a silver tray. He went first to Lorelei, then to Jon, and finally to Coleridge.

Coleridge took his glass and lifted it in Jon and Lorelei's direction. "To your health, both of you," he toasted. But his eyes were fixed on Jon.

"Gracias, mi querido angel," he told the servant as the boy turned to head back to the house.

Coleridge took a long sip from his glass. Then abruptly he rose and moved to a chair directly facing Jon.

"Enough of polite chitchat," he said. "Let's get to the matters that I think we should discuss."

"I'd like that very much," Jon told him calmly.

Coleridge studied Jon for several moments, eyes unblinking. "There was a British general," he began, "who had a motto—'Never explain. Never apologize.' Tonight, however, I'll amend that."

"I don't want an apology," Jon said. "What I do want are answers."

"And you'll have them." Coleridge took a breath; this wasn't going to be as easy as he'd hoped.

"First, I regret Mr. Stagg's behavior. Believe it or not, he is a licensed private investigator. But unfortunately, my associates hired him without fully appreciating the man's character. As you well know, he's shown himself to be a sadist. He also happens to be quite inept at what he does. It was a great mistake to have employed him."

"And why exactly did you—or your associates—employ him? He said it was because I might find out too much about the Audubons."

"Quite the contrary," Coleridge assured him. "Stagg got it all wrong. His instructions were to follow you, yes, but to watch you. That was all. What he did, the birds and the nastiness in

Rivière D'Or, those were Stagg's ideas, and very stupid ones at that."

"You wanted him to watch me for what purpose?" Jon asked.

"To gain information."

"Of what sort?"

"Whatever you've told Brian Ravener," Coleridge said.

A brief, ironic smile followed. "It may come as a surprise to you, but I like Brian Ravener. I understand him. We're birds of a feather, you might say. Tough-minded. Driven. Men who rose from poverty to create successful businesses. *Rich* men, and proud of it. On the other hand, I know that his feelings about me are very different. Most of all, he won't forgive me about Meredith."

"For marrying her?" Jon asked.

"For stealing her away from him is what he claims. But how could I steal what he'd already abandoned?"

"I don't see what any of this has to do with Eddie Stagg," Jon said.

"Just this. Ravener is the prime suspect in Abel Lasher's murder. Many people think he's guilty."

"Do you?"

"No."

"Then who is?"

"I have no idea. But that person knows the art world and the side of it the public seldom sees—the greed and the backstabbing, the perverse pleasure some take in destroying the careers of others so as to enhance their own. Lasher was a master at it, and as a result, made a lot of enemies. It was inevitable one of them would murder him. . . .

"It's true to say," Coleridge continued, "that in that same dirty world, I have enemies as well."

"And you're afraid the person who killed Lasher might try to kill you?"

"Yes. Therefore, to protect myself," said Coleridge, "I wanted to learn what you'd discovered on Ravener's behalf."

"And what have I learned?"

"Very little in detail. But Ravener has given you a list of the four people *he* suspects, and that's a start."

"What was your relationship with Abel Lasher?"

"You mean, were *we* enemies? The answer's no. He was irritating to me in the way an insect is. His bite might raise a welt for a short time, but nothing more. He disliked me, even denounced me, because I have the wealth to buy great art. But all collectors were subject to his scorn, including Ravener. Frankly, I don't blame Brian for trying to beat his brains out at the gallery reception."

"On that subject," Jon said, "did you have a chance to look at the Audubons after Ravener unveiled them?"

"Not really." Coleridge shook his head. "Meredith and I were at the other end of the room when all the fuss began. But from what I could see, they looked well-painted. I particularly liked the Montezuma quail, and the watercolor of the owl feasting on a vole."

Out of the corner of his eye, Coleridge saw Angel approaching them, carrying the tray. The boy stopped a distance from them, lowered the tray and bowed his head to await Coleridge's command.

"Another wine? Lorelei . . . Jon?" Coleridge asked. Both declined. *"Non, gracias, Angel,"* he told the boy and dismissed him.

"To get back to the four Audubons," he went on, "even if they are forgeries, I'm sure Ravener believed that what he was purchasing was genuine. All collectors have been stung from time to time, myself included. It's a risk you take."

Coleridge checked his watch. "Dinner should be ready soon. Afterward, I'll show you some of my more recent acquisitions."

He stood, hands to his hips, the lion tamer once again. Obviously, the discussion of the Audubons was over. Lorelei and Jon stood as well.

"May I enjoy the view a bit more," Lorelei asked, "before it gets too dark?"

"Of course," Coleridge allowed.

She went to the edge of the terrace and looked out, shading her eyes against the rapidly declining sun. Turning back to them, she called, "Is that another garden down below? I didn't notice it when we came in."

Jon and Coleridge walked over to the place where she was standing.

Beneath the terrace, covering a large expanse of slightly sloping ground, Jon saw a formal garden of privet hedges and topiary shrubs, some trimmed in imaginative shapes. Many of the hedges were well over six feet high. As he studied them, he realized they formed a labyrinth of twisting, narrow paths, most of them terminating in dead ends.

While Lorelei and Jon gazed down in silence, Coleridge watched them both, awaiting their response.

Lorelei was first to speak. "It's fascinating."

Coleridge nodded. "But, alas, it has a tragic recent history."

"What's that?" she asked.

"A death."

She looked up, startled. "Whose?"

"The gardener who tended it," Coleridge responded. "He was an old man to begin with, in his late seventies at least. His name was Mario. He took great pride in the garden, caring for it with a passion that a man might lavish on a beautiful woman. A month ago, he worked sun-up to sunset: pruning, cultivating, trimming. He also liked the fact that it was a labyrinth. He took to calling it his *Giardino Labirintho,* his Maze Garden, if you will . . .

"He never worked at night, of course. But that night, he returned to it. He lived in the village with his daughter. It seems he'd lost one of his religious medals that day in the garden and decided to come back to find it. His daughter wanted to come with him, but he wouldn't let her; he knew exactly where the medal was, he said. He'd take a flashlight, he assured her, find the medal, and come home."

Coleridge shook his head. "Unfortunately, he did not."

"What happened?" Jon asked.

The gray eyes lifted, staring into Jon's. "The old man made his way into the garden to the place where he was sure the medal could be found. He was correct; the medal was exactly where he thought. Then, as he started back, his flashlight failed. It was quite dark, there was no moon, and he became lost among the cul de sacs. It seems he fell and couldn't rise. His daughter, meanwhile, slept on, expecting his return. In the morning, when she discovered he was missing, she rushed here. Several of us searched and finally found him. One hand still held the flashlight he'd brought with him. Clutched in the other hand was the medal. And the man was dead. The coroner diagnosed the death as hyperthermia, leading to a heart attack. But it was more than that, I'm sure."

"What do you mean?" Jon asked.

"When we found his body, there was a look of panic on his face. I think he became lost, disoriented, and his terror grew. The garden that the old man loved, the maze of paths and hedges he had tended all those years, had closed around him and imprisoned him. He realized it. And he died of fright."

"How awful," Lorelei murmured softly.

"Yes. It was a pity," Coleridge said. "I was fond of the old man. It demonstrates, however, that there may be unanticipated dangers when one ventures into a labyrinth."

He continued, with a smile to them both, "Shall we go into dinner now?"

THE LIMOUSINE STOPPED before the entrance canopy of the apartment building at Park Avenue and Eightieth Street. The doorman approached it, acknowledging Lorelei and Jon's arrival with a crisp nod.

The moment both were out of the car, the limousine swung back into traffic and sped north along Park Avenue.

"I feel sorry for the chauffeur," Lorelei said, watching the car accelerate. "It's almost midnight and the poor man still has a ninety-mile drive ahead of him."

"At the velocity he's going," Jon said, "he'll exceed the speed of light."

They walked through the set of doors into the building lobby.

"You're welcome to come up and have a drink," Lorelei said. "My friends are probably home by now."

Jon shook his head. "Thanks anyway. But it's been a long

day for both of us, and I could use the walk. The hotel's only a few blocks away."

Lorelei gave him a wry smile. "Do you realize you just spoke three full sentences? That's more than you said during the entire return ride to New York."

"I guess it is. I'm sorry. I was thinking about lots of things."

"Were you? Or were you afraid the chauffeur might be listening?"

"After the experience with Stagg, I wouldn't put it past Coleridge to do something like that, not at all."

"You don't like Myles Coleridge, do you?"

"I don't like him or dislike him," Jon said. "For the most part, I don't trust him."

"Again, because of Stagg?"

"Coleridge claims he hired Stagg to get information from me to protect himself. But I think it was a warning to me to stop asking questions. And there are other reasons I don't trust the man."

"Such as?"

Jon looked around the mirrored lobby. Except for the doorman, who had returned to the front desk, the area was empty.

"Do you recall tonight when Coleridge was giving us a tour of his art collection?" he asked as they walked across to the elevators.

"Certainly. It was impressive. Everything from the Old Masters to a Winslow Homer."

"Do you recall the Goya painting of the child?"

"I thought it was sweet."

"It was. Too sweet." Jon said. "I'm sure it was a forgery."

"Why would Coleridge hang a forgery and call it real?"

"Some collectors, if they own a valuable original, sometimes have a copy of it made to display publicly," Jon explained. "The original is kept hidden in the owner's personal collection, so if a thief steals the one on display, he's taken the fake, not the real one."

He paused, pondering his words. "But I suppose what puts me off about him most is the man's arrogance. He takes pleasure in intimidating people. He's a bully."

"Lots of that could be bravado," Lorelei suggested. "He's overcompensating for what he thinks of as his humble origins. Walking us through his art collection, he was like a little boy showing off his toys."

"Maybe. But some bullies can get very angry, even violent, if anyone does something to their toys."

The elevator doors parted. A couple stepped out, both in formal wear, and headed across the lobby to the street.

"It's very late. I better go," Lorelei said.

While Jon held the elevator doors, she gave him a quick kiss. "Thank you for the evening."

"Thanks for coming with me."

She smiled. "I'm honored. No one else I know has had a private tour of The Aerie."

"By the way," he asked, "do you know what the word 'aerie' means?"

"A high place where a bird roosts," Lorelei said. "That would describe Coleridge's estate."

"Yes," Jon said. "But there's another meaning to the word."

"Which is?"

"A feeding place for birds of prey."

12

AS THE LARGE, barrel-chested man in the red vest neared the conclusion of his imitation of the wood thrush, the other members of Save Our Songbirds murmured with delight. SOS, as it was called, was an organization dedicated, in the words of their charter, "to the appreciation, preservation, and propagation of the native songbird." Comprised of about sixty people, the group met once a month in a residence of one of their members—in this case, the large living room of a townhouse in the West Seventies.

For his part, Jon wondered if he'd been right to accept an invitation to address the gathering. But years ago, when he'd come to love birds and devote his art to them, he'd pledged himself to do what he could to foster an enjoyment and understanding of them. Even if it meant sitting through an overlong recital of birdcalls performed by a two-hundred-fifty-pound man with a chest that seemed capable of swelling to the proportions of a male frigate bird at mating time.

The man ended with his tour de force—the bobolink in spring—and the gathering broke into applause. As the clapping diminished, the group's chairwoman thanked Mr. Bunshaft for what she called his "dazzling display of avian arias."

The chairwoman now turned to Jon. Mercifully, her introduction of him was unflowery and brief. When she was done, Jon rose and moved to a lectern adjacent to a screen. Facing the screen was a slide projector on a table a short distance away. He made his own brief introduction to the group, then signaled to another woman at the far end of the room to dim the lights.

The woman moved to a panel of switches beside a set of double doors.

At that moment, one of the doors opened and a young blond girl in an ankle-length white dress stepped into the room. She took a chair in an unoccupied row nearest the doors and sat down. The lights faded.

Jon spoke for twenty minutes, illustrating his remarks with slide reproductions of his paintings of various songbirds. When he was finished, the lights were restored and the audience applauded.

"Now, I know a number of you have questions," he continued. "I'm told you placed them in a basket in the hall as you came in. If I may have that basket now, I'll read as many of your questions as I can and try to answer them."

He nodded again to the woman at the end of the room. She disappeared into the hall and returned with a shallow wicker basket containing a quantity of index cards. She carried the basket to Jon. He put it on the table next to the slide projector and picked up the card that lay on top of the pile.

" 'In what way,' " he read aloud, " 'would you say your paintings of birds differ most from those of Audubon?'

"The major one," he said, "is that Audubon was an artistic

genius and I'm not . . . but speaking practically, it's in our different methods of working. I paint mostly from sketches or photographs of live birds in their natural environment. Audubon frequently painted from freshly killed birds, many that he himself had shot, which he mounted and wired into lifelike poses to give them the appearance of vitality and movement."

He glanced down at the basket briefly to select another card. What he noticed tucked into the side of the pile was not an index card, but a folded slip of paper. Intrigued, he withdrew it, unfolded it, and read what had been written:

> *Urgent we talk about the fake Audubons. When you leave here, meet me at Strawberry Fields. I also know who killed Lasher.*

There was no signature.

Jon looked up at the audience. He saw that all eyes were on him, waiting for the question to be read.

He hesitated, searching for a plausible response. "I believe," he told them, "that I've already answered this in my slide presentation, so I'll go on to the next question."

He reached to the basket for another index card, while at the same time, slipping the folded piece of paper into a pocket of his slacks.

As he lifted the card to study the question before reading it aloud, he heard a soft click. His eyes darted to the far end of the room just as one of the doors closed.

The chair where the blond girl in the white dress had been sitting was empty.

IT HAD BEEN no more than a section of uneven ground, most of it grass and low shrubs, at the western edge of Central Park. Then, in May 1984, John Lennon of the Beatles was fatally shot outside his apartment building directly across from Central Park West. In Lennon's memory, the patch of land was made into a garden and given the name of Strawberry Fields, after the song "Strawberry Fields Forever" that Lennon had composed.

It was after nine o'clock when Jon left the West Side townhouse of the bird group and headed to the park. At Seventy-Second Street, he crossed Central Park West and walked toward the arching trellis at the entrance to Strawberry Fields. The wisteria vines covering the trellis were in bloom, and he could smell their pungent scent as he approached.

He turned onto the path and stopped at once. Yards ahead, the girl stood, her white dress and blond hair visible against the intertwining vines. Even in the darkness, there was something familiar about her, as if they'd met briefly in the past.

"Hi," was all she said. Her voice had a fey, breathless quality. "You came."

"You seemed certain I would."

"I was," the girl said.

"How long have you been here?"

"After I saw you read my note, I left the meeting."

"That was almost an hour ago," Jon said. "You came directly here?"

"Yes."

The idea of her waiting in the dark, enclosing archway troubled him. "Why don't we go sit on a bench along the avenue?" he suggested.

"No. I'd rather stay in the park."

"Central Park can be a dangerous place if you run into the wrong people."

"Any place can be dangerous if you run into the wrong people."

"At least, let's walk down to the park drive," he offered. "We can sit by the lake."

"Okay."

In silence they started down the path leading to the connecting roads that wound around the park. Along the broad walks bordering it, people strolled, enjoying the pleasures of the summer night.

Crossing the park drive, they found an empty bench that looked out on Central Park Lake. Across the surface of the water, luminous streaks of yellow shimmered, reflecting the ring of streetlights encircling the lake.

Finally, the girl broke the silence. "I lived on a lake once," she said. Her words had the halting, wistful quality of someone waking from a dream.

"Where was that?" Jon asked.

She turned to him. "Where was what?"

"The lake. You said you once lived near a lake."

"Yes." She turned from him again to stare out at the water.

"Where was it you lived by a lake?" he repeated.

"Minnesota."

"What's your name?" he asked.

The girl shook her head. "It doesn't matter."

"Then tell me how you knew where to find me tonight. You're not one of the members of the bird group, obviously."

"No."

"But you got into the room and left that note."

"I told the woman outside I was new. When nobody was looking, I slipped the note into the basket."

"Where I'd be sure to find it."

"Yes."

Along the walk in front of them, some teenagers swept by on skateboards, shouting to each other and high-fiving as they went.

"You said you had some information for me," Jon reminded her.

"I do."

"So?"

"How much?"

"How much what?"

"How much is it worth to Ravener to know who forged the Audubons?" She faced him suddenly. "How much? Half a million?"

"I don't know."

"Then call him. Ask him what it's worth to him to know who did the forgeries. Also, who killed Abel Lasher. Ask him."

Jon proceeded cautiously. "A half-million dollars is a lot of money."

"Not to buy back a life."

"Whose?"

The girl didn't answer, but turned back to the lake. Around them in the softness of the evening, fireflies winked languidly. Beyond them, in a tree beside the lake, an owl could be heard, its call as mournful as a lamentation for the dead.

"Whose life?" Jon asked again.

Her answer was a whisper: "Mine."

"Even if Mr. Ravener agrees to pay you for the information, how can he be sure it's true?"

"The night of the reception at the Wide Wharf Gallery," the girl said. "You and your girlfriend were there."

"How do you know that?"

She ignored his question and continued gazing at the lake. "Lasher said one of the paintings on the wall, the quail, was also called a 'fool's' quail, and only a fool would have bought it thinking it was real."

Jon realized she had the words almost exactly. "What happened after Lasher stepped up on the platform?" he asked.

"Ravener grabbed him and threw him against a wall. Lasher said he'd sue, and Ravener said 'I'll kill you first.' "

"You seem to know a lot about what went on that night," Jon told her. "Were you at the reception, too?"

"There were lots of people there that night. But I know what I know."

A couple ambled past them, talking quietly between themselves. Jon waited until they'd reached the transverse road before he spoke.

"If Ravener agrees to pay for the information," he asked, "how do I get back to you?"

"You don't. I'll contact you. You're at the Hotel Stanhope."

"Yes, I'm staying there," he said.

"I'll call you in the morning."

"What time?"

"Seven-thirty. It's the only time I can."

She stood as if to go. Jon also rose.

"Seven-thirty. I'll wait for your call."

"Otherwise, I'll have no chance." She paused and looked at him. "I may not anyway."

"What do you mean?"

Instead of answering, she turned and ran in the direction of the transverse road.

In the tree, the owl called.

"HALF A MILLION!" Brian Ravener was incredulous. "For that amount, she *better* have good information."

"I think she does," Jon said. He stretched out on the bed in his hotel room. It was almost eleven and he realized now how fatigued he was.

"Either she was at the gallery on the night of the reception," Jon went on, "or she's close to somebody who was."

He heard a sigh. "All right," Ravener conceded. "Let's say I agree to pay her, then what?"

"She said she'd call me in the morning. Seven-thirty. When she does, I'll work out a way to get the money to her in exchange for whatever evidence she has."

"Hard evidence, yes, and not some cockamamy story she made up to rip me off," Ravener insisted. "She'll want cash, too, I'm sure."

"Probably. I'll know a lot more when I talk to her tomorrow."

"But if she does have solid information," Ravener said, "it'll be the first break in the case we've had. The police are still coming up with zero on Lasher's murder. How are you doing with that list of people, by the way?"

Jon glanced over at the investigators' file that lay open on the bedside table. "I'm working my way through it, but I haven't learned much. I've already seen David Bethune and Diana Cardigan. I've also left a couple of messages on Jack Briscoe's answering machine. So far, no luck—he hasn't called me back."

Ravener grunted. "I can't imagine you'll get much, even if you do catch up with him. Just between us, I consider him more a poseur than a real artist. He zips around from one art party to another like a water bug. As far as talent, he's a competent technician and that's all."

"Sounds like you know him fairly well."

"Not really. And I don't own any of his pieces. Once or twice Ariel's suggested that I buy one, and she's sold several of his paintings in her gallery. When she learned he'd be at his Nantucket beach house on the day of the reception, she invited him. . . . Anyway, keep trying to reach him," Ravener continued. "Something may turn up. And call me in the morning after you've spoken with the girl."

"I will."

"What time did you say she'd call you?"

"Seven thirty," Jon said.

"Seven thirty," Ravener repeated.

THE SMALL GREEN numbers of the bedside clock blinked.

7:54 A.M.

Jon had awakened early, as he always did in summer. But instead of dressing in a T-shirt and his running shorts and going for a jog in Central Park, he'd ordered breakfast in his room, then read *The New York Times,* occasionally glancing at the clock and waiting for the telephone to ring.

Seven-thirty had arrived without a call. By seven-forty-five, he'd felt the first deep stirrings of concern, but tried to put them from his mind

Seven fifty. Twelve floors below, along Fifth Avenue, the klaxon siren of a fire engine could be heard passing. Brakes squealed and horns honked.

Still, Jon sat beside the telephone, staring at the bedside clock. It now said 7:55.

He grabbed up the phone and tapped in the number for the hotel message desk. He heard a click.

"This is Jon Wilder," he said and gave the number of his room. "Have there been any calls for me, last night or earlier this morning, that I might have missed?"

"I'll check," the voice said. Another click. A pause. Then, "No, sir. There's been nothing."

"Thanks," Jon answered. He hung up.

7:56.

How long should he wait? Another hour? Two?

7:57.

He decided he would wait till nine. Then he would contact Brian Ravener and tell him the girl had not called.

To pass the time, he picked up the remote control of the television set and snapped it on. The screen came instantly to life. On it, an anchorwoman for a local station was concluding her report:

". . . as yet unidentified. But the victim was in her late teens or early twenties and was wearing a white dress at the time her body was discovered, according to police. Anyone who can provide further information is asked to call— "

Jon turned off the set. Concern had turned to dread.

13

JON STOOD IN the lobby of the Stanhope reading the copy of *The New York Post* the concierge had given him. The article confirmed what he had feared.

> MODEL'S BODY FOUND IN HUDSON
>
> A 20-year-old woman was found dead early this morning under an abandoned Hudson River pier at the foot of Barrow Street. The discovery was made by teenage boys who had gone to the pier to swim. The victim was identified as Mimi West, who, police said, had been employed as an artists' model. According to a preliminary autopsy report, the woman had been strangled.

Jon was about to put the newspaper aside, when he glanced at the next paragraph. It stopped him.

> Although police will not confirm the information, a suspect in the crime is David Bethune, an artist who is known to have seen the victim yesterday

Suddenly, Jon knew why the girl had seemed familiar; he'd seen the portrait of her when he'd visited Bethune's loft in the afternoon.

Jon looked around the litter-strewn alley that led in from Wooster Street alongside the Scorpio Gallery. At the far end of the alley, against a wall that housed the gallery, was a rusted metal door covered with spray-painted names and images in vivid colors. FLASHMAN! appeared in letters a foot high; also the WOOSTER WEIRDOS, and RIKKI RIKKI RIKKI, in Day-Glo orange script.

Jon knocked on the door. There was no answer.

When he'd called Bethune's number from the hotel, the telephone had been picked up by a police officer. Jon had rung off at once. His first thought was that Bethune was in police custody or being questioned as to what he knew about the girl's death. But maybe not. Since Bethune wasn't at his loft, Jon thought he knew the place the man might have gone. He'd decided to give it a try. He'd left the hotel, found a taxi, and provided the address on Wooster Street.

Jon knocked on the metal door again.

"David, it's Jon Wilder," he said in a low voice. "If you're there, I'd like to talk to you. I'm alone; no one knows I'm here. Maybe I can help you."

There was a shuffling behind the door; a lock was disengaged. The door opened slightly and Bethune's face appeared. "Come in."

Bethune opened the door, allowing Jon to enter, then closed it at once and locked it. The room in which they stood was small: a combination storage room and office that included a desk, around which boxes had been stacked.

Bethune turned to him. "How did you find me?"

"When we talked yesterday," Jon said, "you told me you had an opening here in a few days. Half an hour ago, I called your loft and the police answered. You weren't there, so I took a chance you might be here."

"Yes. The gallery owner gave me a key. When the police arrived at my building in the middle of the night, I panicked. I slipped out a back way and came here."

Bethune started for an opposite door that opened into the gallery. "Let's talk in the back room. It'll be easier."

Jon followed him into a rear exhibition room. Hung around the walls were oils and pastels, most of them nudes in a variety of poses. On tracks above the walls were tiny spotlights. None was lighted, but a skylight in the center of the sloping ceiling cast a milky glow. The room was connected to a larger one that faced the street.

Next to a wall was a low stepladder, which Bethune offered. "Have a seat—unless you'd prefer a chair."

"No. This'll do." Jon sat down, straddling it.

At the same time, Bethune made a circuit of the room, glancing furtively in the direction of the front gallery.

"I won't turn on the lights, if you don't mind," he said. "A part of this room can be seen from the street, and I don't want anyone to know we're here."

"That's fine with me."

Abruptly, Bethune stopped before him, looking down at him. "You said you could help me."

"Maybe," Jon said. "If you tell me about Mimi West."

"I didn't kill her."

"I don't think you did."

"The police do," Bethune said.

"Why? Because she was at your loft yesterday?"

"Yes." Bethune took a long breath. "Other reasons, too."

"Tell me about her," Jon urged.

Bethune began to pace again. "I've used her as a model for about a year."

"That's a pastel of her, isn't it?" Jon pointed to the portrait of a nude girl reclining on a bed.

"Yes. I did that one a month ago. I think it turned out rather well."

Jon stood and stepped closer to the painting. Even in the half-light of the room, the skin tones were luminous. The girl's hair was long and blond and curled loosely at her shoulders. She lay indolently, staring back at the observer with somnolent, seductive eyes.

"It's very good," Jon told Bethune.

"Thank you. But as a model, she was wonderful. And it was more than just her physical proportions, which were perfect. She radiated a naivete, a purity."

He gave Jon an ironic glance. "She was neither naive nor pure, of course. Far from it. But when she posed, those qualities were what one saw, in spite of what she was doing to herself."

"What was she doing to herself, as you put it?"

"Drugs mostly. Alcohol. I also assume she had a rather active sex life. I'd heard stories."

"Did you know much about her background?"

"Very little," Bethune said. "Apparently she came to New York City several years ago from Minnesota, hoping to become an actress. To support herself, she started waiting tables in the Village. Then one day an artist saw her and asked her if she'd model for him. She agreed to."

"Who was the artist? Do you know?"

"No. But she was a natural; she took to it at once. And other artists took to *her*. Soon lots of them were asking her to pose for them, and she gave up the waitress job."

Bethune leaned closer to the painting, studying it intently, as if for the first time. "A tragedy, a death like hers. She was so beautiful."

"You said she was at your loft yesterday."

Bethune turned back. "That's right. In the afternoon." He paused. "As she was leaving, though, she made a strange request. She said she planned to see someone in the early evening. But she asked if after that, she could come back to my loft and spend the night. She said she'd sleep on the chaise longue."

"Why did she want to come back to your place?"

"She never told me. But it was as if she was afraid of someone."

"Who?"

"I have no idea," Bethune said. "But I suspect it was the person she was living with. When she asked to stay at my place, there was a desperation in her voice."

"But you refused her."

"Yes." Bethune gave a look of sad regret. "Now I wish I'd let her stay. If I had, she might still be alive." He hesitated, avoiding Jon's eyes. "As it was, a friend was staying for the night."

"When we talked earlier," Jon said, "you were certain the police suspected you of killing her."

"Because I'd given her the check. But there was more to it." Bethune began to pace again. "When we were finished yesterday, I paid her, as I always did, by check. It was too late for her to take it to the bank; she said she'd cash it the next day.

"Then she asked for some cocaine; she'd called earlier that day to make certain I had it on hand. I generally don't do cocaine, but it'd been a long day . . ." He let his voice trail off.

"So when she and I were done, I put some on a glass-top table, rolled up the check I'd given her, and she sniffed the coke through the check like it was a straw. I did the same, but not as much."

"And you're afraid she was carrying the check when she was found."

Bethune nodded. "When we were done, she put it in the pocket of her dress. It had my name imprinted on it. If the police tested the check, and if the coroner found traces of cocaine in her system, it follows they'd come after me."

"This person she lived with—did she ever talk about him? Use his name?"

"No, none of that. Except one time she mentioned he was fond of 'hoisting a pint.' I guessed that was his phrase, not hers. It made me think that he was British."

JACK BRISCOE'S APARTMENT was on Bleeker Street.

Crossing Wooster, Jon walked to Prince, then headed west. In the first years of their marriage, when he and his young wife were art students, they had lived in this part of the city. Since her death, Jon had been reluctant to return—afraid, perhaps, of being haunted by the ghosts of bittersweet recall.

But today the ghosts spared him, and he felt only a nostalgic wistfulness as he revisited the streets: Thompson, Sullivan, MacDougal, and the others he remembered with such fondness. Of the old buildings, many still bore familiar signs—Madam Olga, Reader and Advisor; Patsy's Shoe Repair; Kolosky's Kosher Foods.

On Bleeker Street, he found Jack Briscoe's building, a modest brownstone indistinguishable from the others on the block. He climbed the steps to the front door. The apartment listed for J. Briscoe was on the second floor. Jon pressed the bell beside the name and leaned down to the intercom, hoping to hear Briscoe's voice.

There was no response. He pressed the bell a second time. Still nothing. Either Briscoe wasn't home or wasn't answering. Jon headed down the steps and walked toward Washington Square Park.

He was almost to West Fourth Street when he saw McGivney's Public House. It looked exactly as it did years ago, when it had been a favorite gathering place for Jon, his friends and fellow students. The name, with the large shamrock in bright green, still hung above the door. Jon again remembered Briscoe's brief allusion to McGivney's during their chance meeting in New Elysium several weeks ago.

He pushed open the door and stepped inside. It was as if he had transported back in time. Everything was just as he remembered it—the bar of polished oak that ran the length of the front room, the gleaming brass foot rail at its base; the bar stools with their well-crushed, dark-red leather seats; the mirrored wall behind the bar against which bottles sat in regimental rows.

Wooden tables occupied the center of the room, with booths along the right and at the rear. Standing at a table, a red-haired waitress with a lilting brogue chatted with a young man. Another, smaller room was visible in back. At the moment, half the tables appeared occupied, as were the booths. At the far end of the bar, two construction workers put their hard hats to one side and signaled to the man behind the bar.

Francis J. McGivney caught their sign and began filling two pint mugs with Harp draft beer.

Jon smiled to himself. Of all the memories associated with McGivney's, its owner seemed to have changed least. His hair, which had been prematurely white when Jon had known him, was still carefully combed into a pompadour. The broad, round Irish face (Irish as Paddy's pig, the man was fond of saying of himself) still had the fleshy smoothness and the reddish flush. The flush made many wonder if McGivney was a heavy drinker. *Was,* the man took pride in telling everyone. A raging alcoholic in his youth, he had been sober now for forty years, attending weekly meetings of Alcoholics Anonymous with the same devotion that he gave to Sunday masses at St. Margaret's Church. He'd even offered the rear room of McGivney's as a place for A.A. meetings, a suggestion that was gratefully but speedily declined.

The man delivered the two Harps to the construction workers, turned back and saw Jon standing at the door. A toothy smile spread across his face.

"Dear Blessed Mother! Is it who I think it is?" McGivney said.

Jon started toward the bar. "Jon Wilder . . . how are you, Mac?"

A beefy hand thrust out. "How many years has it been? Fifteen? Sixteen?"

"More like twenty, I'm afraid." Jon shook the hand.

"You haven't aged a day. Well, maybe one or two. I'm noticing a bit of gray above the ears."

"A bit and then some," Jon agreed.

"And how's that pretty young thing you were sweet on? I heard the two of you got married and moved up to Connecticut. And had a daughter, too."

"Yes." Jon paused. "They both died. In an accident."

McGivney looked at him, then bowed his head and shook it. "I'm so sorry, Jon. I mean that," he said finally. "She was a lovely girl. I'm so sorry."

"Thank you."

"Can I get you a drink? Lunch also—on the house."

"Maybe some coffee." Jon pulled up a bar stool and sat.

Mac raised an index finger. "Without sugar. Just a drop of milk."

"You still remember that."

McGivney poured the coffee, briefly adding milk, and set it before Jon. "I hear you're painting birds now."

"Yes."

McGivney laughed and swept a hand around the room. "Then come, particularly on the weekend, and you'll find some pretty strange birds here—the girls dressed like peacocks, and the young men, bantam roosters showing off . . ."

He turned away to fix himself an iced tea in a tall mug, then returned to Jon. "So, what is it that brings you to the Village?"

"I was in town," Jon told him, "and happened to be in the area. I suppose you still get artists stopping by?"

"Some, yes," McGivney answered. "But the artists these days aren't the same. Would you believe, some are even painting on *computers?* Michelangelo is probably spinning in his grave."

"What about the artists living in the neighborhood? Do they come in?"

"Again, some do," McGivney said. "Name names and I can tell you."

"What about a painter named Jack Briscoe?"

The man frowned and sipped at his iced tea. "Funny you should mention him."

"How so?"

"He's what I'd call a regular. Comes in here once or twice a week."

"What sort of person is he?"

McGivney frowned a second time. "He strikes me as a phony; he puts on more airs than an Irish folk-song festival. Look at the la-di-da accent and gold chains. And then there's the dark glasses. Briscoe's very touchy when it comes to the dark glasses."

"Touchy in what way?"

"He wears them all the time," McGivney said. "I thought it might be on account of some medical condition, like being oversensitive to light. As it was, a month ago Briscoe happened to be sitting alone in a back booth, and this drunk keeps looking in his direction. Finally, the man goes over to Briscoe. He asks, kidding-like, if Briscoe is a movie star, or one of the Blues Brothers, on account of the dark glasses, don't you know.

"Briscoe tries ignoring him, but the guy's really into it. He asks Briscoe if he's Stevie Wonder in white-face, or if he's collecting for the Lighthouse for the Blind, and if so, where's the tin cup and the cane. Suddenly, Briscoe stands up, grabs the guy's shirt and smashes him across the face. It took me, the cook, and three customers to get Briscoe to stop hitting him. Otherwise, I think he would've killed the man."

"What happened then?"

"The guy runs out, blood all over him, shouting Briscoe broke his nose."

"And Briscoe?"

"Cool as a cucumber, the fact is. Started in with the apologies to everyone, didn't know what got into him, so very sorry for the row, and all of that. What it showed me was that Briscoe has a short fuse. Light it and you could have one hell of an explosion on your hands."

McGivney gestured to Jon's coffee cup. "Another?"

"No, thanks. What else can you tell me about Briscoe? How long has he lived in the Village?"

"Six or seven years, I'd guess."

"And before that?"

"Couldn't say." McGivney shrugged. "Is he a friend of yours?"

"Let's say I'd like us to get reacquainted. How recently has he been in?"

"Last night he was."

"Last night?"

"About eleven. Frankly, I suspected he'd been drinking. Still, he was his chatty self, glad-handing everybody in the room. The girl he was with was just the opposite. Tense. All the time looking toward the door."

Jon leaned forward on the bar. "Was she Briscoe's girlfriend?"

"I couldn't tell you. Lots of women seem attracted to him, the mystique of the artist and all that. Briscoe introduced her, but I didn't catch the name. This place gets sort of noisy at night."

"What did she look like?"

"Young. And very pretty."

"Blond?"

"Yes."

"Do you recall what she was wearing?"

"Indeed I do," McGivney said. "A long white dress. I even complimented her on how it looked—I thought maybe that might cheer her up." He set down his glass of iced tea, "Wait, now—her name. As they were leaving, Briscoe called her 'Mem,' or something like that."

"Could it have been Mimi?"

"Could be. Her last name was a short one also."

"West? Was her name Mimi West?"

"Mimi West, that sounds right. Hey—" McGivney halted, his eyes staring into Jon's. "Wasn't that the girl who was murdered?"

"Yes, it was," Jon said.

14

Carrying the small suitcase he'd brought with him to New York, as well as mail from his post-office box in Scarborough, Jon went directly to his study. A late-afternoon breeze had come up on Seal Island Sound, spreading whitecaps across the water.

He put the mail on the desk. As he did, he noticed that the green light of the answering machine was flashing. He pressed the "Play" button and listened. The first call was from Lieutenant Lydecker; he wanted Jon to know, he said, that a toxicology report confirmed that a fast-acting industrial toxin, carbofuran, had been used to poison Jon's birds. The second message was from Lorelei, asking him to call her at the shop when he returned. The last call was from Malachi La Tour, who said he had some news for Jon about the Audubons, and to telephone him when he had the chance.

Jon phoned the Scarborough police and thanked Lydecker for his information, then telephoned Lorelei's antiques shop and found she had just left. When he called the number Malachi La Tour had given him, he discovered he'd reached the

Straus Center for Conservation, part of the Fogg Museum in Cambridge, where La Tour had said he hoped to test the four Audubons.

"Hi, Jonny," La Tour said when he came on the phone. "I have news for you. As you suspected, Ravener's Audubon Quartet is very much off-key. No question the paintings I picked up from him are forgeries. The experts at the Straus are going over them with me tomorrow. I'd like you to be here, if you can."

"You bet. What time?"

"Eleven."

"I'll be there."

After La Tour gave him directions, Jon thanked him and rang off. He picked up the phone again and tapped in a number he found in his address book.

"Ravener," the voice said at once.

"Brian, it's Jon. Sorry to call you on your private line, but I have some information for you about the Audubons, the ones you gave to Malachi La Tour. They're definitely fakes. The experts at the Straus Center tested them. I'm driving up to Cambridge in the morning to get the results."

"I can't say I'm pleased to hear it," Ravener acknowledged, "but the news doesn't come as any shock. What time will you be here?"

"Eleven. That's what La Tour suggested."

"Come for dinner, then."

"Thanks. Can we make it on the early side?"

"How's six?"

"That's fine." Jon added, "Will it be just the two of us? I mean, will Ariel be there?"

"No. She's on Nantucket all this week. Why do you ask?"

"Only that it'll give us a better chance to talk if we're alone."

"That's true." Ravener agreed. "Six then. I'll tell Mrs. Ferris to expect you."

"Speaking of Ariel," continued Jon, "you said she's on Nantucket?"

"Yes. She's putting together a new gallery show. I'll be seeing her this weekend, though. I'm flying down."

"Jack Briscoe has a beach house on Nantucket, doesn't he?"

"Somewhere off Polpis Road. In Quaise. But what does that have to do with Ariel?" Ravener was curious.

"Since I haven't been able to reach Briscoe at his New York apartment or his studio," I thought Ariel might have seen him on the island recently."

"Well, the two of them are acquaintances to some degree, I told you that. She may know where to find him. When I talk to her tonight, I'll ask."

"Thanks." Jon heard a small click on the phone. "Brian, are you there?"

"Sorry." Ravener said after a moment. "That was Ariel; I've got her on call-waiting now. I'll see you tomorrow night."

"See you then," Jon said and hung up.

He leaned back in his chair and began to look through the assorted mail on the desk. Among it was a large manila envelope that was marked "Photos—Do Not Bend." The sender was identified as Peter Swift. The "Peter" stopped him briefly, until he realized that it was probably Pesky's real name.

Jon slit open the envelope and carefully withdrew the contents. As he expected, it was a set of color photographs of birds that Swift had told Jon he would send. On cursory examination, they were quite good, and more sensitive than Jon would have expected.

There was also a separate, smaller envelope. A handwritten

note from Swift said that along with the bird photographs, he was including several candid shots he'd taken at the Wide Wharf Gallery the night of the reception. Among them were photos of David Bethune and Wilson Tyne toasting one another, Myles Coleridge glaring at the camera, and one of Jon and Lorelei together, taken the moment after Swift had confronted them. Jon's eyes were wide and he had a look of startled wonder on his face.

The next photograph was a close-up of Jack Briscoe. He was smiling broadly, the lights of the gallery reflecting off the surface of the dark glasses. The person upon whom he was lavishing his charm was a pretty, dark-haired woman in a saffron evening gown. For her part, she seemed to be regarding Briscoe with an expression that seemed less spellbound than perplexed, as if to say: "You've told me who you want me to believe you are. But tell me, really, *who are you?*"

Staring at the photo, Jon found himself asking the same question. Who are you, Jack Briscoe? Really.

Jon went to his suitcase and took out the investigators' report. He turned to the dossier on Briscoe. The first time he had read it, he'd skimmed over Jack Briscoe's early life. Now he studied the report more carefully, jotting on a pad significant details and events.

According to the report, the man was born John Edward Briscoe on June 7, 1942. He grew up in London's East End, the only son of working parents. His father was a drayman for a brewery, his mother a domestic. When he was still a baby, both parents were killed during a blitzkrieg bombing of the city. He was taken in by an aunt and uncle on his mother's side, and went to live in Ashford, Kent. At the age of nineteen, and having shown promise as an artist, Jack, as he was known, returned to London, where he enrolled in the National Institute of Art. He graduated from the institute in 1964. His first employment was with the graphics design firm of Begbie and Muldow, in Islington.

Jon moved to the next paragraph of the report. It mentioned a New York City gallery show in which Briscoe was one of a dozen artists whose works were on display. Following it, there were shows in San Francisco, Dallas, Chicago, and Miami Beach. Specific galleries were also mentioned, as well as several prominent collectors who had acquired Briscoe's work. One of them was Myles Coleridge. Simon Kreutzer was another.

Jon noted the names of the galleries and the collectors. He was about to read on, when he realized there was a detail he had missed. The year of that first gallery show in New York City was 1988. The shows in San Francisco and the other cities followed it at later dates.

The report contained nothing about Jack Briscoe from the time he had left the National Institute of Art in 1964 to the New York show in 1988—a span of more than twenty years. Where he'd lived during those years, how he'd earned a living, whether he had had exhibitions of his paintings, there was not a word.

But seeing Simon Kreutzer's name among the purchasers of Briscoe's paintings gave Jon an idea. He flipped back to the report on Wilson Tyne, found the number of the Kreutzer Museum, and called it. When a young man answered, Jon identified himself and asked to speak to Tyne. A moment later, Tyne was on the phone.

"Hello, Jon . . ." Tyne's voice sounded cautious. "It's not about David Bethune, is it? The police have already been in touch with me."

"Actually, it has to do with Briscoe. The day you and I spoke outside the museum, he showed up with a large abstract that had been bought for the museum."

"I remember," Tyne said.

"My question concerns Briscoe's background."

"Oh?"

"Does the museum have some sort of biography on him? A resumé? Since Simon Kreutzer has bought several of his works, I thought the museum's files might include one."

"Let me look," Tyne said.

He was back in a short time. "I have something, but it isn't much. Briscoe was born in London in—let's see—1942. He was orphaned the same year and adopted by an aunt and uncle in Kent. In 1961, he enrolled in the National Institute of Art and left there three years later."

There was a pause as Tyne presumably perused the information. He continued, "After that, I see a list of gallery shows, beginning with New York."

"Does it indicate when he came to the United States?" Jon asked.

"Not that I see."

"The New York City show you mentioned—is there a date?"

"Yes—1988." Another pause. "That's strange . . ." Apparently Tyne had spotted the same gap in time.

"There's nothing listed between 1964 and 1988," Tyne noted. "But of course, as a young artist starting out, he may have had to go into another line of work."

"Maybe," Jon agreed.

"That's about all I can tell you," Tyne concluded. "I'm afraid I haven't been much help."

"On the contrary," Jon said, "you have."

They exchanged good-byes. Jon hung up and turned back to the report on Briscoe. Tyne's information on the man confirmed what Jon had realized: there were no details on Jack Briscoe's life for those intervening years.

Had Briscoe married? Raised a family? If he had traveled, where? Had he abandoned art as a career and tried another occupation? Nothing in the public record on him gave a clue.

Then something flickered in Jon's memory. Colin Hightower had once mentioned the National Institute of Art. But in what context, Jon couldn't recall.

He picked up the telephone again and tapped in the number of the shop.

"Hightower Woodworking," the answering machine message announced in the familiar rotund tones, "Our business hours are from—"

"Colin, it's me," Jon cut in. "If you're there, could you pick up? Otherwise, I'll—"

"Jon . . . what is it, dear boy? I'm about to close the shop."

"This may seem like an odd question," Jon said, "but at one time or another, you mentioned the National Institute of Art in London."

"I did. As a young man, I attended it."

"You were a student there?"

Colin snorted. "Don't sound so surprised. I've been told I have a modicum of talent in the arts."

"I mean, that's wonderful."

"On the other hand, don't overdo it," Colin said. "A simple 'I agree' will be enough."

"What I mean is, maybe you can help me. What years were you there?"

"The early fifties," Colin said. "I was a cheeky lad at that age, supremely confident of my own artistic genius, and convinced that with a bit of training, I was destined to become the next Constable or Turner. Then, after I graduated, I discovered that my true medium was wood, not paint. So I put aside my paint palette and canvases and picked up the chisel and the awl."

"But since you're a graduate, do you have some kind of an alumni directory? Anything that would list others who might have been enrolled?"

Colin pondered. "I believe so, yes. If I do, it would be upstairs with my books. I was just about to go up to fix dinner for the cat and me. Give me a few minutes and I'll call you back."

"If you do come across it," Jon said, "there's a name I'd like you to look up. He would have graduated with the class of 1964."

"Indeed. And what's the name?"

"Jack Briscoe."

"Let me see what I can find."

"You're fortunate, my friend," Colin stated straightaway when he called back. "I found an alumni directory for the Art Institute. It's current, but I don't believe I've looked at it. Bear with me . . . Jack Briscoe, you say?"

"Yes."

Jon could hear pages being turned. "B-B-B-B," Colin repeated to himself. "Bl-Bo-Boyle . . . I knew a Jimmy Boyle once." More pages turned.

"Ah, yes. Here we are. Brinson . . . Brisbane . . . Brisby . . . *Briscoe!* I have it!" Colin paused. "Or not. The directory shows listings for two Briscoes. The first is Daphne Briscoe, and unless your Jack has had a sex change, I suspect he/she is not the one you want. The other is a J. McNaughton Briscoe. It's closer. J could stand for John or Jack. But he graduated from the institute in 1939, which would make him around eighty. Again, not the person you're looking for, I fear."

"No," Jon answered. But the information didn't come as a surprise. "Thanks for checking anyway."

"Wait, now," Colin told him. "There's a section at the back they call 'Necrology.' That's the academic word for dead. I can check that if you like. But it's a long list and a lot of graduates have necrolized."

"Don't bother," Jon said. "This Jack Briscoe—or whatever his real name is—was alive as recently as last night."

For that matter, Jon thought, so was Mimi West.

15

JON ARRIVED IN Cambridge at ten-thirty, parked in a garage on Harvard Street and walked the several blocks to Quincy. The Straus Center—officially called The Philip A. and Lynn Straus Center for Conservation and Technical Studies—was on the fourth floor of Harvard's Fogg Art Museum. Within it were workrooms and laboratories with the most sophisticated technological equipment for the examination and preservation of works of art.

As Jon approached the entrance to the Fogg, he saw Malachi La Tour in animated conversation with a young black man. La Tour caught sight of Jon and waved.

"Good morning, Jon," he said as Jon joined them. He added, to the young man, "Daryll, I'd like you to meet Jon Wilder. Jon, this is Daryll Washington. Daryll received his doctorate in art history this May. Top honors."

"Congratulations," Jon said, shaking the young man's hand.

"Thank you, sir. And thank you, Dr. La Tour, for your advice." He offered his good-byes and headed in the direction of the university.

La Tour watched him go. "I enjoy working with young people," he said. "It's payback for all the help professors gave me during my student years." Then he turned to Jon. "So, shall we have a look at the Audubon Quartet?"

He opened the door for them to enter the museum, then started down a corridor, with Jon following.

"The watercolors have been undergoing tests since we received them," he continued. "Microscopy, ultraviolet, betaradiography. Also chemical analysis. Now that all the tests are done, the paintings can be returned to Ravener."

"I'll be seeing him this evening," Jon said. "I can bring them to him then. By the way, who did the examination?"

"Several people," La Tour said. They arrived at an elevator. He pushed the "Up" button, "The conservators for paint and paper each had a look, as well as their assistants. The final examination of them was done by Dr. Vanderkamp."

"Who's he?"

"She," La Tour corrected. "Dr. Gertrude Vanderkamp. She's the duenna of art conservation. She also knows the works of Audubon. I studied under her when I was a graduate student at the Fogg. Except, she never uses the title "Doctor." Also, she refuses to be addressed as Ms. *Miss* Vanderkamp is what most people call her, but she lets me get away with Gert. She's a nononsense person, as you'll see; some people say she's too brusque, but I adore her."

The elevator halted at the fourth floor and they stepped out. La Tour continued down a hallway to a door. He opened it and stepped aside to let Jon enter. The room was small and brightly lit with a long wooden table in the center. At the end of the table was a slide projector directed at a screen that hung against a wall. Along the length of the table, the four Audubon watercolors had been laid side by side.

But what drew Jon's attention in particular was the tiny woman in the red dress who stood on the near side of the table. She was in her seventies, he guessed, with gray hair tied into a bun. Rimless glasses perched above a prominently jutting nose.

Malachi La Tour went to her and kissed her lightly on the cheek. "Good morning, Gert. I'm delighted you're involved in this."

The woman gave him a genuine, if fleeting, smile. "I'm always pleased to be of help to you, Dr. La Tour."

"I'd like you to meet my friend, Jon Wilder," La Tour told her. "Jon, this is Gertrude Vanderkamp."

Jon shook the woman's outstretched hand. "Miss . . . Vanderkamp. How do you do?"

"I've looked forward to meeting you," she said. "I'm an admirer of your bird paintings, although you tend to use too much blue to suit my taste. But perhaps that's because you live near the water."

From the corner of his eye, Jon could see La Tour's wry look. "Thank you," Jon told Dr. Vanderkamp. "And you're probably right about the blue."

"Let's get to the business at hand," the woman said.

She moved along the table, waving a hand over the paintings with her fingers spread, as if providing an appraisal of them through her fingertips.

"As Dr. La Tour probably told you, Mr. Wilder, these watercolors have been examined scientifically as well as by the human eye, my own and others. There's no doubt that they're fakes. Any questions before we begin?"

"Just one," La Tour said, raising his hand. "How recently would you say these forgeries were done?"

"Quite recently," she answered. "That is, within the year." Her eyes darted to Jon.

"Any questions, Mr. Wilder?"

Jon shook his head. "No." Under her gaze, he felt as if he were back in school.

"All right, then. Let's begin," she said.

She tapped the table in front of the watercolor nearest them. "Here we have a painting of the Lawrence's goldfinch. The others are a spotted owl eviscerating a vole, a sage sparrow, and a Montezuma quail."

Turning to the slide projector, she flipped a switch. There flashed onto the screen a series of horizontal lines that appeared raised, as if magnified under a microscope.

"First," the woman said, "I draw your attention to the paper. The forger painted on paper of high quality; by that, I mean paper composed of linen and cotton fibers with very little surface texture. It's close to what Audubon himself used, except that our tests show it was produced in the late nineteenth century."

"In other words," La Tour suggested, "it's paper that was manufactured after Audubon died."

"Exactly." Vanderkamp rewarded him with a brief nod of approval. "To have used this paper," she went on, "Audubon would have had to be well over ninety years of age. And we know he died when he was sixty-six."

"But how did the forger get the old paper?" Jon asked.

"Probably by visiting antiquarian bookshops and buying old and very large art books. What he did was to remove the blank endpapers and use those on which to paint.

"Now let's address the matter of the paint and the painting technique employed in these forgeries," she continued.

She pointed to the watercolor of the Lawrence's goldfinch, then changed the slide. Displayed on the screen was a close-up of the bird's wing. The streaks of yellow had been highlighted with gold.

The woman turned to Jon. "I gather it was you, Mr. Wilder, who first detected the use of gold metallic paint."

"Yes," Jon acknowledged.

"Very good." She bestowed the same approving nod on Jon. "And there were other things that we detected inconsistent with Audubon's technique."

She picked up the watercolor of the Montezuma quail. "Notice the white markings on the quail's face. The white paint is heavily applied. Sometimes Audubon *did* use white that way to cover his mistakes. But mostly he depended on the white reserve of the paper itself, scraping away the wet watercolor paint to show the white of the paper below."

Two more slide images flashed onto the screen in rapid succession. The first showed an extreme close-up of the quail's eye with the white paint surrounding it; the second, the head of Audubon's painting of an Atlantic puffin, where the white reserve was visible.

"Excuse me, Gert," La Tour said, "but if that painting of the quail was a genuine Audubon, wouldn't the lead in the white paint have turned to gray or black by now from oxidation?"

"That's correct," Dr. Vanderkamp agreed. "This paint is far too new."

She replaced the quail with the others on the table. "One more thing. Take a close look at these four together. Come on. Bend down and tell me what you see."

Jon and La Tour did as they were told, bending over the watercolors, scrutinizing them at closer range.

"If these were real Audubons," Jon said, "you'd notice a certain burnishing of the paper and the media itself, a kind of surface crust."

"And why is that?" she asked, once more the schoolmistress seeking to draw answers from her students.

"Because Audubon stored his paintings flat in stacks," Jon suggested. "The burnishing occurred when a sheet was dragged across the underlying piece. These paintings don't show that."

"Bravo, Mr. Wilder," she answered. "In addition, something about these paintings just isn't right; an ingredient is missing. Audubon's special artistry, perhaps. These paintings are competently done, but not by Audubon. And I'm sure the forger never thought they'd be subjected to the examinations that our people put them through."

"Thanks, Gert," La Tour told her. "And thank your people, too."

"I have a question," Jon said. "Given the techniques you uncovered in these paintings, do you have any idea who the forger might be?"

"There are a few clues; idiosyncracies," the woman said, "that bring to mind a forger who was active in the seventies. He also had a fondness for gold metallic paint."

La Tour's eyebrows lifted. "Do you really think it's him?"

"Perhaps, perhaps not," she admitted. "Nonetheless, it's an intriguing thought."

"It's hard to believe he's resurfaced after all these years," La Tour told her.

"Excuse me," Jon put in, "but I'm not as knowledgeable in

the world of art forgery as you two. Does this man—this forger—have a name?"

"Indeed he does. Or did," said Dr. Vanderkamp. "The name was Breen."

"WHO'S BREEN?" JON asked La Tour as soon as Dr. Vanderkamp had left the room.

"A forger who was convicted in the nineteen seventies," La Tour explained. "At the time, it was a rather celebrated case."

"Tell me."

La Tour looked at his watch. "I'll tell you that it's also noon. There's a place nearby that serves good fish and chips. You game?"

"Sure," Jon said. He gestured to the watercolors on the table. "But what about these?"

La Tour began gathering them. "You told me you were seeing Ravener tonight. I'll put them in a box and leave them at the security office of the Fogg. That way, you can pick them up any time you like."

Jon gave him a sardonic smile. "Considering that Ravener had an armored car transport them to and from Nantucket, having me deliver them by cardboard box is something of a comedown."

La Tour returned the smile. "But considering they're worthless fakes, I'd say hand-delivery is special treatment. Let me find a box."

Twenty minutes later, both men were seated in a booth at Mistress Quickly's, a small restaurant close to Harvard Square that sought to match the decor, if not the dress and customs, of Elizabethan times.

"So was I right?" La Tour asked, popping a French fry into his mouth. "A plate of fish and chips and a good pint of ale, and your trip to Cambridge has been worthwhile."

Jon put down his tankard of ale. "What's made it worthwhile is learning what I did from Dr. Vanderkamp. Tell me more about Breen."

"Jeremy Breen." La Tour leaned back in the booth and repeated the name slowly. "Jeremy Breen. What do I remember? It was a while ago."

"You said he was convicted in the seventies."

"Seventy-seven was the year, I'm sure of that." La Tour looked up. "I was in my last year of graduate school at the Fogg."

"What do you recall about him?"

"He was British."

"Tall? Short?"

"Average height, I'd say."

"What about a physical description?" Jon asked. "Beard? Mustache? The color of his hair?"

"Clean-shaven, I think. Dark-haired, too," La Tour added. "Although the photos of him in the newspapers were black-and-white."

"How old was he then?"

"Mid-thirties, probably."

"Which would put him in his fifties now," Jon said.

He reached into an inner pocket of his jacket and drew out the candid photo of Jack Briscoe that Pesky Swift had sent.

"Take a look at this." Jon placed the photo on the table facing Malachi La Tour.

"Who is it?" La Tour studied the photo.

"An artist named Jack Briscoe. It was taken at that Nantucket reception several weeks ago. Does he look anything like Breen?"

La Tour picked up the photograph, then set it down. "I couldn't say," he answered finally. "This fellow's bearded with gray hair. Also, Breen didn't wear dark glasses, I'm quite sure."

Jon tapped the photo with a finger, leaving it before La Tour. "Even so, the man has aged. And couldn't some of that be part of a disguise?"

"Explain."

"I think that after Breen got out of prison," Jon said, "he changed his name and altered his appearance. What *didn't* change was that he went back to his old profession."

"Of art forgery." La Tour bent to the photo again. "Possible . . . it's possible," he granted Jon.

"And that would account for all the missing years."

Jon summarized the report on Briscoe that the investigators had collected; specifically, the gap in time between Briscoe's presumed graduation from the London art school in 1964 and the next mention of him as part of a gallery show in the U.S. in 1988.

"What I find curious," Jon said, "is why he kept the same initials, J. B., when he took an alias."

La Tour shrugged. "Maybe he had monogrammed luggage he was fond of."

"Tell me more about Breen's trial," Jon asked. "Where did it take place?"

"Right here. That's why I remember it." La Tour popped another French fry in his mouth.

"Really? Here in Boston? What time of the year was it?"

"Early spring," La Tour said. "I'm not certain of the day it began, but I recall the day it ended—the first of April, April

Fool's Day. I know, because after his conviction, a reporter asked Breen if he had a statement. Breen stopped, glowered at the man and said he did. He said it was significant that he was found guilty on April Fool's Day, since everyone connected with the case—judge, jury, prosecutor, even his own lawyer—was a fool."

"Who brought the charges against Breen in the first place?" Jon asked.

"An art dealer with a gallery in the Back Bay," La Tour said. "Pantelli was his name."

"Do you remember the details?"

"Vaguely, yes." La Tour took a deep swallow of his ale. "The art dealer had agreed to buy some forged works Breen was attempting to pass off as Picasso drawings. As the two men were concluding the deal, Breen became suspicious that he was being set up and flew into a rage. Bottom line: Breen physically attacked the man. When the indictment came down, it wasn't just for forgery and fraud."

"Was there another charge?" Jon asked.

"There was." La Tour set down his mug and looked at Jon. "Attempted murder."

JON SLID THE chair forward and slowly twisted the dial of the viewing machine. Gradually, the image on the screen in front of him became distinct.

At the top he saw the newspaper's masthead, *The Boston Globe,* and below it, the date: Thursday, March 24, 1977.

After leaving Malachi La Tour, Jon had driven to the public library on Boylston Street and gone directly to the section where back editions of Boston newspapers were kept on microfilm. He'd asked the clerk, a sallow young man with a ponytail, for the newspaper accounts of a trial that had taken place in Boston in the spring of 1977. Jon had added that the last day of the trial had been April first, but that he wasn't certain when the trial had begun. Offered both the *Globe* and the *Herald*, Jon chose the *Globe*.

Together he and the clerk had settled on the date of March 19, two weeks prior to the conclusion of the trial. The first three rolls of microfilm, containing the editions from March 21 through 23, had offered nothing.

Now Jon began to scan the edition for March 24.

The article appeared on the second page of the section that contained local news. "Fireworks Mark First Day of Forgery Trial," read the headline. The "fireworks" referred to was a scene sparked by the defendant, Jeremy Breen, when he struggled with one of the court officers he claimed had mishandled him.

The first two days were devoted to the selection of the jury. The real business of the trial began on Monday, March 28. The charges against Breen were repeated: fraud and attempted murder. Breen's chief accuser was a man named Carlo Pantelli, the owner of an art gallery to whom Breen had sold the forged Picasso drawings, and the person Breen had allegedly attacked. According to the article, the attorney representing the defendant was a man named Leonard Crane. The state prosecutor was identified as Karen Stolley. To Jon's disappointment, there was no photograph of anyone associated with the trial.

The profile of Jeremy Breen presented by the prosecutor and the defense attorney could not have differed more. The state depicted Breen not only as a forger and a charlatan in passing off the faked Picasso drawings as genuine, but also as a dangerous psychotic with a homicidal personality. Breen's attorney, on the other hand, described his client as an honest man, albeit overtrusting of a friend who'd owned the drawings and who'd asked Breen to sell them on his behalf.

The first witness for the prosecution was Carlo Pantelli himself. Under direct examination, he recalled meeting Breen six months earlier, on October 20, 1976. On that day, Breen had walked into his gallery and offered to sell twelve pen-and-ink drawings by Pablo Picasso. They had been owned, Breen told him, by a close friend, who needed money to pay off some debts. With the drawings came a letter of authenticity, Breen added, signed by Picasso himself. The asking price was $150,000.

Looking at the drawings, which were figures out of Greek mythology, Pantelli found them charming and consistent with Picasso's early style. Still, he asked Breen if he could hold onto them for a few days to study them at greater length. Breen was initially reluctant, but agreed. In fact, Pantelli now admitted from the stand, something about the drawings made him dubious; what it was, he wasn't sure. The next day he showed them to a friend who was an expert on Picasso's works. The colleague took one look at them and judged them to be "wrong"—the euphemism in art circles for forgeries. He urged Pantelli to contact the police.

When Pantelli did so, the Police Fraud Division saw an opportunity. They offered to install a hidden camera in the gallery and asked Pantelli to proceed with the transaction, pretending to believe the drawings were authentic. They also asked Pantelli to wear a listening device so as to record Breen's remarks. When Breen returned to the gallery on the appointed day, Pantelli gave him a cashier's check for $150,000 and received the forged Picassos and the letter in return.

Then something happened.

Either Breen caught sight of the hidden camera or the listening device Pantelli wore. He became verbally abusive; he accused Pantelli of tricking him, and hit him with his fist. Then, before Pantelli could respond, Breen grabbed a small bronze figurine and began beating him about the head. Pantelli shouted. The commotion brought one of his young assistants running from the back. At that, Breen fled the gallery.

In cross examination, Breen's attorney sought to discredit Pantelli's testimony, pointing out inconsistencies between the statement he'd given to the police immediately following the incident and what he'd said today. But Pantelli stuck to the details of his story, and blamed any earlier misstatements on his disturbed state of mind following the beating he'd received.

The second prosecution witness was the gallery assistant who had rushed to help Pantelli at the time of the assault. The assistant described the ferocity of the attack, adding he was sure Breen would have killed Pantelli, given half a chance.

The next day the prosecution introduced its evidence—the twelve forged drawings Breen had sought to sell. A trio of art experts testified that they were fraudulent. But the most damning evidence was the videotape made by the hidden camera in Pantelli's gallery. In graphic images, it showed both the sale of the forgeries and the savage beating of Pantelli. Together with the words and sounds recorded by the listening device, Breen's guilt seemed irrefutable.

The case for the defense came as an anticlimax. Leonard Crane spoke of his client as a fine painter in his own right, but too trusting of a friend. The friend, Crane told the courtroom, was one Armand Desjardin, on whose behalf Breen had attempted the sale of the Picasso drawings without questioning their authenticity.

What the police did after Pantelli went to them, said Crane, amounted to entrapment. If Breen displayed anger, it was the reaction of a man against such entrapment, nothing more. Concerning witnesses for the defense, Crane offered none, including Breen himself. Crane's only success appeared to be arguing down the charge of attempted murder to one of aggravated battery.

The closing arguments were presented on the afternoon of Thursday, March 31. Jon scrolled through the microfilm accounts of it and found little information that was new. The one exception was the prosecution's statement that Breen's so-called friend, Armand Desjardin, had not been located by either Interpol or the French police, and in all likelihood, was as mythical as the characters on the Picasso drawings.

Jon picked up the last roll of microfilm and inserted it in the viewer. The account began on the front page of *The Globe.* At 9:00 A.M. on Friday, April 1, the judge gave his instructions to the jury, and the twelve men and women retired to deliberate. They returned three hours later with a verdict: guilty on both counts. Throughout the procedure, Breen sat stone-faced and mute.

It was the calm before the storm.

The storm broke immediately following the trial, just as Malachi La Tour had said. When asked by a reporter for his reaction to the verdict, Breen thundered with apocalyptic wrath. He reminded everyone that it was April Fool's Day, and went on to denounce everyone connected with the trial as a fool or worse.

The story was continued on an inside page. Jon scrolled to it now.

Suddenly he saw what he'd been hoping for—a photograph of Breen and his attorney, surrounded by a crowd outside the court. It had the grainy quality of most newspaper photos, yet still conveyed a fleeting moment in time, forever frozen by the camera lens.

Reaching for the dial that adjusted the magnification, John focused on the photograph, enlarging it until Jeremy Breen's face filled the screen. His hair was dark, the face clean-shaven; he wore no dark glasses. Otherwise, the features Jon knew very well. It was the face of Jack Briscoe twenty years ago.

Ironic and appropriate, thought John. Breen, the master forger, had achieved the ultimate in forgery—he had forged himself with such success that as his own counterfeit, Jack Briscoe, he had been able to deceive the world.

Jon was about to rewind the microfilm when something made him stop. He leaned forward to the screen again and stared at Jeremy Breen's face. What was it about the photograph that troubled him?

Then he knew.

It was the eyes. In the bright lights of the television cameras, the left eye appeared sunken in its socket and out of alignment with the right. While the right eye glared angrily into the camera, the left eye pointed blindly into space.

Jon also knew the reason: he'd had an uncle who, in family photographs, had had the same peculiar look.

Jeremy Breen had a prosthetic eye. The dark glasses Briscoe always wore were more than just an affectation, they were a necessary element in his own reinvention, and a vital part of his disguise.

16

THE BELLS OF Trinity Church chimed four o'clock as Jon crossed the street to Copley Square. Before leaving the library, he had checked a telephone directory. Of the two numbers he sought, he had found only one.

He located a bench where the traffic noise would be less insistent. Taking the small cellular phone from an inside jacket pocket, he tapped in the number.

"Duffy, Masefield and Crane," a woman's voice said at once.

"Good afternoon. My name is Jon Wilder. I'm seeking information on a court case that took place twenty years ago. I believe one of the attorneys, Leonard Crane, represented the defendant."

There was a pause. "I'm sorry, sir," the woman said. "Leonard Crane has passed away. But his son Philip is a senior partner. Perhaps he could help you."

"I'd appreciate it. Please."

After a brief pause, a male voice answered, "Mr. Wilder? Crane here. I understand you asked about an old court case my father was connected with."

"Yes. In the spring of 1977, your father represented an art forger who—"

"Jeremy Breen," interrupted Crane. "I remember the case well, I'm sorry to say. May I ask your interest in it, Mr. Wilder?"

"I'm a friend of Brian Ravener—" Jon began.

"As am I," Crane said. "Well, we're not close acquaintances, but we belong to the same club. I have great admiration for the man." There was a pause. "I gather he's in quite a nasty fix right now."

"I'm trying to help him out of it," Jon said. "So any information your office can provide about the Breen case might have a bearing."

"Well, it's all a matter of public record, anyway," conceded Crane. "What would you like to know?"

"Were you involved in the case yourself?"

"No. But I know enough about it from my father's accounts. He wished he'd never met the man. I'm sure the whole experience hastened my father's death."

"In what way?"

"His health declined rapidly after the trial; Breen put him through a lot. My father died less than a year later." Crane added, "Hold on—let me get the file."

Jon waited, listening to the sounds of drawers being opened and papers being shuffled.

"Here we are," Crane said when he returned. "Now, what would you like to know?"

"A few things. First, do you have any idea of what happened to Breen after he was released from prison?"

"None." Crane said. "I can tell you that without looking at the paperwork. Soon after his release, we tried to contact him concerning some follow-up legal matters, but the man simply disappeared. We concluded that he'd left the country and returned to England. What else can I tell you?"

"The Pantelli Gallery was in Back Bay, but I couldn't find a listing for it in the telephone directory," Jon said. "I suspect it's out of business."

"And has been for some years. But there's another gallery at the same address," Crane volunteered. "It's called The Forecastle; it sells nautical paraphernalia, mostly. I do a bit of sailing and I've been there once or twice. Maybe the owner has some information on Pantelli that we don't. I'd check with him."

"I will," Jon said. "Just one last thing. Do you have any idea if Breen worked alone? I mean, was there ever any thought of an accomplice?"

Philip Crane was silent for a moment. "Interesting that you should mention it," he said. "My father questioned Breen about it, too. Breen stuck to his story that there was no one else. But my father didn't believe him."

"Why?"

"Because Breen knew far too much about how Pantelli ran the gallery—the man's schedule, where he kept his records, things like that. Breen also knew Pantelli was suspicious of the drawings."

"Was the accomplice someone working in the gallery?"

"That was my father's supposition, yes." said Crane. "Pantelli employed two young men and a young woman. On the evening of the confrontation between Breen and Pantelli, none of the assistants should have been there. It was after hours and the gallery was closed. The three had left together a short time earlier."

"But I thought one of the assistants went to Pantelli's rescue when Breen started to beat him."

"Quite true," Crane agreed. "As I told you, the assistants had just gone for the evening. Then one of the young men remembered something that he'd left behind. He returned and was in the rear office when Breen arrived at the front door. Pantelli let Breen in, the argument followed, the assistant heard the shouts and rushed into the room. That's when Breen fled.

"I'll add one thing," continued Crane. "Pantelli must have also suspected Breen had help from someone working in the gallery. A week after the trial ended, Pantelli fired the two other assistants."

Jon's hopes rose. "Would you have the names of those assistants?"

"Possibly. Again, hold on while I look."

Jon heard a thump at Crane's end as the phone was set down, followed by sounds of more papers being riffled. Crane picked up the phone again. "Yes indeed," he said. "Names and addresses both. Of course the addresses are from twenty years ago. God knows what's become of the people now."

"I understand." Jon tucked the phone between his ear and shoulder, took the pen and notepad from his pocket, and prepared to write. "Let's start with the names."

One by one, Crane read the names of the assistants while Jon wrote them on the pad. At the third name, John caught his breath. My God, he thought. He stared down at the pad.

"That's about it," Crane concluded. "Mr. Wilder . . . are you still there?"

"Yes—excuse me," John said. "Thank you for the information."

"I hope I've been of some help."

More than you know, Jon told himself.

WHILE THE OWNER of The Forecastle concluded a sale to a young couple who were purchasing a framed print of a British man-of-war, Jon took the time to look around the gallery.

As Philip Crane had told him, the building in which Carlo Pantelli had once maintained his business was now occupied by a shop that specialized in nautical art and antiques. The walls were painted in a soft rose tone. Against one wall hung lithographs of brigantines and schooners, their sails billowing, as well as legendary ocean liners from the past—the *Lusitania,* the *Normandie,* the *Ile de France.* Inside glass showcases there were collectibles, including scrimshaw, a number of ships in bottles, vintage yachting caps, a pair of polished marlinespikes, and wooden Jack-tars carved by sailors on long voyages to while away the days.

The couple left the gallery, and the owner, a short, jolly man in his late sixties, came over to Jon.

"Welcome to The Forecastle," the man said. "My name is Frederick Quince. Is there something in particular you're looking for?"

"Information, mostly," Jon said. He introduced himself.

"I'll try," Quince said. "Do you mind if we sit down?" He gestured to a pair of deck chairs in a rear corner of the room. Approaching them, Jon saw they were of polished wood, obviously old, but well made.

"Would you believe these are from the first-class deck of the *Titanic?"* Quince asked with obvious delight. He eased himself into one of the chairs and extended his legs on the raised footrest.

"My grandfather was the captain of a merchant ship that found them in the North Atlantic months after the liner sank. It gives me a great sense of history to sit in them. But there's a practical reason, too. I just had a hip replaced and I don't like standing for too long."

He inclined his head to Jon. "But you said you wanted information. May I ask what it concerns?"

"It has to do with the art gallery that used to be here."

Quince gave a confirming nod. "Ah, yes. The one owned by Carlo Pantelli. What is it you'd like to know?"

"Until what year was he in business here?"

"Let's see . . . I took over the lease in the early eighties," Quince recalled. "Eighty-two, to be exact. At the time, I had a gallery in Marblehead, but wanted something in the city; Back Bay or Beacon Hill."

"Had you known Pantelli before then?"

"By reputation only," Quince allowed. "His was one of the better Boston galleries. Of course, he dealt in fine-arts pieces, unlike me."

"But you knew of the court trial in which Pantelli was involved."

"The one against the forger? Yes indeed," Quince said. "The trial caused a bit of a sensation in the Boston art community at the time. After I got to know Pantelli, he told me some of what he'd gone through. It was awful."

"What do you mean?"

"I know the whole experience unnerved Pantelli totally. He was afraid that when the forger—what was his name? Breen—got out of prison, he'd come back and finish what he'd started."

"You mean, assault Pantelli again?"

"I mean, kill him. Breen was a crazy man. He seemed capable of such an act."

"Do you have any idea where I could reach Pantelli now?"

Quince shook his head. "No, I'm afraid not. After he sold the gallery, he moved to Italy. He lived in Rome a while, then moved to Tuscany and I lost track of him. I wrote several letters, but they all came back stamped "Addressee Unknown," or the Italian equivalent. I have no great faith in the Italian postal system, anyway. So I stopped writing."

"Do you have any of Pantelli's records?" Jon asked. "Those concerning the gallery, I mean."

"A few. I held onto the tax records for some years. When they were no longer needed, I got rid of them." Quince smiled. "I kept the list of his best customers, of course."

"Do you know anything about the three assistants who were working for him at the time he was attacked?"

"Very little. One of them, a young man, probably saved Pantelli's life."

"And the other two? I understand Pantelli fired them."

"There were rumors that one of them had been in league with Breen," the man confirmed. "In the case of the young woman, it was said that she was in bed with Breen as well. That's about as much as I can tell you . . . no, wait. I do remember one thing." Quince leaned forward on the deck chair and reached to touch Jon's arm. "There was a painting."

"What sort of painting?"

"It was meant as a joke, really," Quince said. "His assistants gave it to Pantelli on his birthday, several months before the incident with Breen."

Quince pushed himself upright, straddling the chair. "It was an oil, and quite clever. It gave Pantelli a great laugh."

"What was the subject?" Jon asked, increasingly intrigued.

"It was a parody of Manet's 'Luncheon on the Grass.' Manet titled it in French, of course— *'Le Dejeuner sur l'Herbe.'* A friend of one of Pantelli's assistants painted it. The figures in it were the same as in the Manet, but the faces were those of the assistants themselves. I found it in the basement when I bought the gallery. Pantelli didn't want it at that point. But it was well painted, and the thing also amused me. So I put it in a storage closet in the rear. It's probably still there."

"You mean you have it?"

"I haven't looked at it in years. But I'm quite sure I do."

"May I see it?"

"If I can find it, certainly." Quince pushed himself up out of the deck chair and headed toward the back.

A short time later, the man reappeared, carrying a small canvas in a wooden frame. "Here we are," he announced. " 'Luncheon on the Grass,' American-style, circa nineteen seventies. In this case, the artist called it 'Brunch on Boston Common.' "

Quince raised the painting, holding each side of the frame. As he had described it, the work was a parody of Edouard Manet's famous work. Missing from the background was the figure of the woman washing in the stream. But in the foreground, just as in Manet's original, two young men and a woman sat amid the trees. Near them, lying open, was a picnic basket from which cheeses, bread, and fruits spilled out. The young men were fully clothed and both wore beards.

The young woman, on the other hand, was nude. She stared directly at the viewer, her right hand to her chin, her large eyes set wide apart, her lips voluptuous and sensual.

It was a face that Jon knew very well. Although the woman in this painting had aged twenty years, she was still beautiful, the smile still provocative, the eyes as compelling and inscrutable as when they had looked into Jon's just weeks ago.

CARRYING THE LARGE, flat cardboard box, Jon mounted the steps of Brian Ravener's townhouse. He pressed the bell and stepped back, expecting to confront the face of Mrs. Ferris. Instead, the door was opened by Ravener himself, dressed in chinos and a T-shirt.

"I saw you getting out of your car," Ravener said. "Come in." He looked down at the box. "Otherwise, my neighbors will think you're delivering a pizza." He beckoned Jon into the foyer. "The difference is that a pizza has more value than what's in the box now. And it's edible."

Ravener took the box from Jon's hands. "I gave Mrs. Ferris the night off," he explained as he led the way toward the kitchen. "But I've already begun to fix our dinner."

"You're a pretty good chef, as I remember. What are you preparing?"

"I call it my Hail Caesar salad," Ravener said. "Not exactly what Caesar himself served up to his legions, but it's tasty."

They entered the kitchen at the rear of the house. Ravener placed the box on a table in a corner of the room and indicated a high stool near it where Jon could sit.

The kitchen itself was large and airy, with tile-covered countertops and suspended from the ceiling, a circular rack from which copper pots and cookware hung. Laid out along one counter there was a head of romaine lettuce, part of a roast chicken, a wedge of Parmesan cheese, an egg, a bowl filled with croutons, and a cruet of dressing. Next to them was a nearly empty wineglass.

Ravener pointed to the glass. "I've already started on a wine spritzer. Will you join me?"

When Jon agreed, Ravener took a second glass from a cupboard, retrieved a bottle of chardonnay and Pelligrino water from the refrigerator, prepared the wine spritzer and handed it to Jon.

Then he refilled his own glass and raised it in a toast. "To Jonathan McNicol Wilder—ornithologist, bird painter, and forgery debunker without peer."

Jon raised his glass. "Thanks. But the real detective work belongs to the people at the Straus."

"I give you a great deal of the credit nonetheless."

"You're certainly in a good mood tonight."

Ravener smiled. "I guess Ariel has that effect on me. I just spoke with her at the gallery. I told her you'd be here tonight and she sent her fond regards."

"Then she hasn't been to Boston recently?"

Ravener shook his head. "With the summer people pouring into Nantucket nowadays, she's kept pretty busy."

He put aside his wineglass and seized the head of romaine lettuce, tearing it apart with his large hands and dropping the pieces into a colander.

"By the way," Ravener said as he worked, "I have some news for you. Do you recall my mentioning a friend who's close to the police commissioner? He told me today they'd found the weapon that killed Lasher."

"I thought Lasher was strangled."

"He was. By a piece of picture wire," Ravener explained.

"Thin, but very strong. The kind artists use to hang their paintings."

"Where was it discovered?"

"On the ferry itself, under one of those big boxes on the deck where life preservers are stored. The police think the killer tossed away the wire after strangling Lasher. But instead of falling into the water, it was blown back onto the deck by the wind, and it ended up under the box."

Ravener took the chicken breast and placed it on the cutting board. "So, tell me about your day at the Straus."

"First, let me ask you a question," Jon said. "Do you remember anything about the trial of an art forger that took place in Boston in the late seventies? The forger's name was Breen."

Ravener thought for a moment, then shook his head. "Only vaguely." He picked up a knife and began slicing the chicken breast. "A lot of other things were going on in my life then and I didn't give it much attention. The forger was found guilty; I remember that."

"On two counts," Jon informed him. "He was convicted of fraud and for assaulting the owner of the gallery. After he was released from prison, he dropped out of sight."

Ravener glanced over his shoulder, continuing to slice the chicken. "What are you suggesting?"

"That about ten years ago, Breen resurfaced under another name."

"Which is?"

"Jack Briscoe."

The knife stopped in mid-stroke; Ravener looked startled. "The same Jack Briscoe who was at the gallery reception?"

"Yes."

Ravener put down the knife, turned and leaned against the

countertop. "So you think it was this Breen, or Briscoe, who forged the Audubons and substituted them for the originals?"

"That's my guess."

"Unbelievable," was all Brian Ravener could say. For him, too, the pieces of the puzzle were beginning to fall into place.

In the far corner of the kitchen, the wall telephone began to ring. "Would you like me to answer it?" Jon offered.

Ravener shook his head. "No, it's all right. It's probably Mrs. Ferris checking to make sure I'm managing without her help."

He went to the telephone and grabbed it up. A look of surprise and puzzlement spread across his face.

"Uh . . . yes, you're right," he said into the phone. "Unexpected is the word . . . no, it's all right. Jon Wilder is here. I'm doing dinner for the two of us." He smiled to himself. "You're right. The Hail Caesar salad. You remember that . . . so, ah, how are you? Good. And Myles?"

Jon moved off the stool and edged toward the door to give Ravener some privacy, but Ravener waved to him to remain.

"I see . . ." continued Ravener into the phone. "How am I doing? Under the circumstances, I'm all right. Remember the African saying I had hanging on my office wall? 'It takes many spears to kill the lion.' Well, I've taken lots of spears in the last few weeks, but not enough to bring me down." He gave a private smile, obviously touched. "You remember that, too, do you? . . . thank you . . . yes, I'd like that. I mean it. I would. Good-bye."

Ravener hung up the phone. "I guess you know who that was."

"Meredith Coleridge?"

"Yes. Calling from Nantucket. She's spending the summer

there, she said." Ravener added, "She also said she'd like to see me."

"Is Myles with her?"

"No. He left this morning, flying off to God knows where. He spends so much time in that airplane of his, they ought to call him Frequent Flier Myles."

Ravener paused, picked up his wineglass again, and sipped. "It sounded as if Meredith really cares about how I'm doing. She said she was concerned after the things she'd heard and read." He shook his head. "Considering what I put her through when we were married, she's about the last person I'd expect to wish me well."

"How so?"

"How so?" repeated Ravener. "Because, looking back, I admit I treated her in shameful fashion; I took her for granted too much of the time. No wonder she left me to marry Myles. . . .

"I guess the gods are smiling on me, though," he went on, "because I have been blessed with the love of two extraordinary women. Meredith was one. The other, as you know, is Ariel. Both women are so different. But in spite of all my faults and failings, which are numerous, I guess they saw some redeeming qualities in me that made them want to take the risk of being Mrs. Brian Ravener."

He fell silent, turning to look out a window that faced onto the rear courtyard.

Jon was silent also. Yes, he thought, they are two very different women. But one of them, my friend, could very soon put *you* at risk.

17

THE NANTUCKET AIRLINES turboprop descended, banking slightly to the left. Jon saw the island a thousand feet below, an enormous delta wing ripped from the mainland by a gigantic hand and flung into the sea. Beyond the sandy margin of its northern shore, Nantucket Sound was visible, its surface smooth as polished turquoise burnished by the morning sun.

The plane continued its descent. Now Jon observed the pair of great stone jetties that extended from the harbor entrance, the lighthouse at Brant Point, then at last the harbor and the town itself, the gray-roofed buildings clustered helter-skelter at the harbor's edge.

Jon checked his watch: ten twenty-five. Soon after his dinner with Brian Ravener the night before, he had driven from Boston to Hyannis and spent the night at a motel adjacent to the airport. This morning he had parked the Range Rover in the airport parking lot, gone to the terminal, and booked a round-trip flight. The flying time between Cape Cod and the island was considerably shorter than the ferry trip had been. The weather, too, was vastly different from the fog he had encountered on the voyage weeks before. The sky was luminously blue, and except for a line of clouds far to the west, the day promised to be hot and sunny. If everything went well and he accomplished what he hoped to, he would fly back to Hyannis late that afternoon, reclaim his car, and be in Scarborough by dark.

If everything went well. . . .

The airplane banked into the landing pattern, starting its approach. Fleetingly, Jon saw bathers and umbrellas along Surfside Beach. The plane slowed further, flared and gently touched the long, broad runway. It continued rolling, turned onto a taxiway, and turned again before coming to a stop outside the terminal.

Moments later, the boarding steps swung outward with the door, then folded down. Jon rose from his seat and joined the other passengers as they deplaned. But unlike many who were headed to the area inside the terminal where baggage could be claimed, Jon sought the public telephones. Locating a Nantucket directory, he verified the address of Jack Briscoe's house in Quaise.

In another section of the terminal, he found an auto-rental agency and booked a Ford Escort for the day. The car was too small for Jon's tall frame, and bright red, not a color he would have selected to help him remain inconspicuous. But with a summer weekend just ahead, it was the only car available.

He drove out of the airport and took Old South Road the short distance to the traffic rotary. Turning east, he continued past the road that led to Monomoy, then swung onto a two-lane winding road toward Polpis and The Moors. He drove for several miles, noting signs for Shimmo and Shawkemo, as well as narrow, unpaved roads with names like Rabbit Run and Fulling Mill. Although the day was warming rapidly, he chose not to use the Escort's air conditioner, preferring to drive with the windows down to feel the wind against his face and smell the pungent salt sea air.

Beyond the Life Saving Museum, he stopped the car at what appeared to be a set of tire tracks meandering off among the reeds. A hand-painted wooden arrow opposite it had been broken in half; only the letters "Qua" were visible. Beside the sign there were three mailboxes set on posts. On the last mailbox he saw the name of Briscoe. Jon pulled down the front flap of the box and found that it was full of mail.

He turned the car into the narrow tracks. Here and there, the reeds gave way to wild grapevines and low, tangled shrubbery. Twice he came to openings that served as driveways to beach houses. At the first, a sign stuck in the sand proclaimed the owner's name: D'Olimpio. The second had a posted notice that unwanted visitors would be greeted by the Messrs. Smith & Wesson.

Without warning, the tracks ended and Jon found himself in a cul de sac of reeds and bushes barely wide enough to turn the car around. He managed it, aware that if he had to make a hasty exit from the scene, the Escort would be pointed toward the road.

He turned off the engine and stepped out. Around him, bulrushes swayed listlessly, as if they, too, had been affected by the sultry languor of the day. Among them, Jon saw a path of hard-packed sand.

Cautiously, he moved along the path for a distance of a dozen yards, ending in a clearing surrounded by beach grass and scrub pines. In the center of the clearing was Jack Briscoe's house. Fifty feet beyond it was the water, and past that, a barren stretch of sand that enclosed it from the sea.

The house itself was small and set on stilts, the outer walls of gray-stained wooden siding. Eight steps led up to a deck encircling the house. On the side facing him, there was a door, and windows across which rattan shades had been drawn.

If Briscoe had wanted someplace where he could hide after fleeing New York City, it was unlikely he would have come here. Even so, Jon walked toward the house slowly, keeping his eyes focused on the windows. He climbed the steps up to the deck. Beside the door there was a padlock hanging from a hasp. The shackle of the lock had been left disengaged. Jon speculated that on the night of the reception, Briscoe had intended to return and had not bothered to close the lock.

The only other security for the house appeared to be in the doorknob itself. Jon saw that it had a simple latch-bolt lock, the kind that could be opened with a credit card. He took one from his wallet, inserted it between the door and door frame and pushed slowly. As he hoped, the bolt slid back. He twisted the doorknob, and the door opened.

The kitchen was the first room he faced. He saw a coffee mug and one plate with a knife and fork sitting in the sink. A dark residue of coffee covered the bottom of the mug. Bits of dry food stuck to the plate, evidence that the items had been unwashed and left for weeks.

Moving on, he saw what served as Briscoe's studio. A large easel stood along one side of it. There was no canvas. On a table, tubes of paint were spread out, and a variety of brushes rested in a row of glass jars, their tips in the air. All were clean and dry.

Jon found the living room, opposite the studio. Along one wall, windows looked out on the water. The room was sparsely furnished: a daybed with bolsters that served as a couch, and several captain's chairs with canvas seats. A coffee table in the center of the room contained half a conch shell that had been fashioned as an ashtray, a month-old copy of *Art Now,* and a large book that displayed a watercolor reproduction of a snowy egret on the jacket. Jon knew the book. It was a recent edition of "The Birds of America," by John James Audubon.

As he was about to leave the room, he caught sight of some things he'd missed earlier. On an end table beyond the daybed were a telephone and an answering machine. The answering machine was disengaged.

Also lying on the table were a notepad and pencil. Scrawled on the top sheet of the pad were two telephone numbers. One began with the 255 prefix, indicating Nantucket. The other number was preceded by an out-of-state area code.

Jon carefully tore off the piece of paper and put it in an inside jacket pocket, along with the pencil. He left the house, locking it as he went out, and walked quickly to his car.

He drove to the road and stopped briefly to check for traffic, leaning forward to see past the set of roadside mailboxes. That gave him an idea. He turned the car, eased up to the mailboxes and folded down the metal door of Briscoe's box. He reached in and withdrew the contents. Flipping through them, he discovered what he hoped to find: a telephone bill. Again using his credit card, he carefully worked open the flap of the envelope and slid out the invoice. On the section that detailed long-distance calls made from Briscoe's telephone in the month before the reception, a dozen calls were to the same out-of-state number that had been written on the pad.

Jon slipped the bill into the same pocket with the piece of paper from the notepad and pulled out onto the road.

THE RETURN TO town was slower than Jon had expected. Milestone Road seemed an endless line of vehicles: cars, trucks, mopeds, and even a few bicycles whose riders scorned the bike path that paralleled the road. It was after twelve when the Escort brought him into town. He parked at the corner of India and Federal, made a brief stop at the post office, and continued on to Hussey Street.

The street was narrower than most, with parking at a premium. But as he drove slowly along it, he saw a minivan vacating a space almost directly opposite Ariel McKenzie's house. He waited for the van to leave, then took the spot at once.

It couldn't have been more ideal; from where he sat, he had a full view of the front and near side of the building.

It was a small, converted carriage house, with a pair of dormer windows extending from a mansard roof. Like many houses on the island, its wood shingles were weathered to a dull gray tone. Beside the house there was a meager area of grass. Because the house had no garage, Jon guessed that the grassy area was where Ariel parked her car. The door that faced the street was plankwood with a black-painted knocker in the shape of a whale. Along the side there was a second door, also of unfinished wood. The windows on all sides were covered by stout wooden shutters that denied passersby a view of the interior.

As to the house's occupants, there was no clue. But Jon was certain there were two of them—Ariel McKenzie and Jack Briscoe.

After killing Mimi West, Briscoe had come directly to Nantucket. Jon was sure of that. Unable to hide safely in his own beach house, he'd come instead to Ariel's. As his lover twenty years ago, when she'd been an assistant at Pantelli's gallery, she'd been his partner in crime. In league with him again over the forged Audubons, she'd given sanctuary to him now.

From behind the wheel of the car, Jon watched the house for several minutes, until it occurred to him that he wasn't sure what he was watching for. If Briscoe *was* inside and hiding, he'd hardly be expected to fling open the windows and announce it to the world.

Rather than remain there, Jon decided on the next and final stop he would make. He turned on the engine and gave a brief glance in the rearview mirror before pulling out into the street.

What he saw chilled him. Coming rapidly up Hussey Street was a white BMW convertible. Ariel McKenzie was behind the wheel.

Jon killed the engine of the Escort and bent down as if searching for something in the glove compartment of the car, praying silently she wouldn't notice him.

Ariel slowed the BMW as she approached her house. She swung onto the grassy strip, leaped out, hurried to the side door and disappeared inside.

She reappeared a short time later, a blue carryall clutched tightly in her hand. She tossed the bag onto the front seat of the BMW and slipped in behind the wheel.

Throwing the car in reverse, she shot backward onto the street. The next instant, the BMW sprang forward, gaining speed.

Jon watched as the car turned at Westminster Street, out of his view. Had he been wrong about Jack Briscoe being in the house? Did the carryall Ariel brought with her mean that she was heading to another place where she could meet him? If so, what would they do then?

There was only one way to find out. Jon pulled the Escort out onto the street and sped in the direction Ariel had taken.

18

WHY SHE HAD chosen to return to the gallery surprised and puzzled Jon. Was he wrong about Ariel's intention to meet Briscoe and her preparations to escape?

But from a distance he observed her as she walked quickly along Wide Wharf in the direction of the gallery, still clutching the blue carryall. For a short time, he lost sight of her among the crowds of pedestrians on the wharf, then saw her as she entered the gallery.

He left the parking lot of the supermarket opposite the wharf, questioning himself again if what he was about to do was wise. The Nantucket police headquarters was a few blocks away. Should he have gone there first and outlined his suspicions? Maybe. But he had no solid evidence. He couldn't prove conclusively that Briscoe had killed Lasher and the girl. Or that Briscoe–Breen had forged the Audubon Quartet.

And where was Briscoe anyway? Jon still believed the man had taken refuge in Ariel McKenzie's house. But that wasn't enough to send the police racing up to Hussey Street in search of him.

Jon had another reason, too, for wanting to confront Ariel alone. She held the key to both the forgeries and Briscoe's whereabouts. But Brian Ravener was very much in love with her. If Jon could speak with Ariel privately and personally and convince her to go to the police, it might soften whatever punishment she could receive. Ravener would feel pain in any case for having been deceived by her. But if Jon could help alleviate that pain in some small way, he owed that to his friend.

He crossed New Whale Street and headed for the wharf. Glancing at the sky, he noticed that long, attentuated fingers of high cloudiness were sweeping in.

Arriving at the gallery, he saw that the door was open. As he stepped in, he was surprised to find the front room very hot. Of the half-dozen people there, several were fanning themselves with the brochure of the artist on display.

Jon walked through to the second room, and found only the gallery assistant, who was rehanging paintings on a wall. Jon went to her and asked for Ariel.

"She's probably in the office." The young woman gestured toward the back. "And I apologize about the heat. The air conditioner is on the blink."

Jon thanked her and moved on to the office in the rear. Looking through the door, he saw another door beyond it, also open, that gave access to a walkway bordering the wharf. He walked to the far door and looked out. What he saw were wooden pilings, several slender masts of sailboats moored against the wharf, and a ladder leading down over the side.

Suddenly a triangle of white began to rise beside the ladder. As it rose higher, Jon observed that it was the mainsail of a small sailboat. He looked down over the wharf and noticed that the lone sailor was a woman. Her back was to him and she was kneeling at the stern, working to unlash the tiller. Near her, on the floor of the boat's open cockpit, was a blue carryall.

"Hello, Ariel," he said.

She spun around and looked up, a hand raised to shade her eyes. She was now dressed in a white T-shirt and shorts, and sneakers without socks. A pair of large sunglasses rested in her hair above her forehead.

"Jon Wilder! What are you doing here?" A smile flashed, identical to the one she'd given him when they'd first met on the night of the reception.

Easy, Jon, he told himself. You're here as a friend. He smiled also. "Do you have a minute?"

"Certainly. But why?"

"I'd like to talk with you."

"I'm honored." Again the smile and the honey tones. "But I hope that's not the only reason for your visit."

"Not the only one. No."

"Well, as you can see, I was about to take a little sail in my boat. I mean, the heat today is so oppressive, don't you think?"

She gestured to the sail that was swinging gently with the wind. "In the summer, I keep her moored here for days such as this. Please. Do come and join me."

"Let's talk here," he said.

"Now, Jon—don't tell me you're afraid to sail with me."

"No."

"Then you can act as my first mate. We'll make a circuit of the harbor and come back. If we haven't finished our 'talk'—which you make sound so serious—we can continue it here."

She patted the ladder that led down to the midsection of the boat. "Come on. Come down."

He didn't move.

Ariel laughed lightly. "Oh, now, Jon—you look uncomfortable. Are you afraid tongues will wag if you and I are seen together in my boat? Come on."

Jon scanned the harbor. Boats continued to crisscross it. On Wide Wharf and the other docks serving the traffic of the busy harbor, people strolled, snapped photographs, or sat on benches looking out. He weighed whatever risks there could be in agreeing to a brief sail in the harbor with her and found none.

"All right," he said at last.

He removed his shoes and socks and placed them beside the ladder. Then he grasped the railings and descended rung by rung until he felt his right foot touch the boat. Moving the leg back, he stepped down onto the cockpit deck.

"Good. You're in," Ariel announced. "If you cast off and push us away, I'll take the tiller."

Jon did as she asked, untying the bowline and pushing off from the wharf so that the boat pointed toward the harbor. While he took a seat along the deck on the port side, Ariel sat at the stern and drew her sunglasses down over her eyes. Then she gripped the handle of the tiller with both hands.

"I'll head toward Monomoy," she said, nodding toward the far side of the harbor. "Myles Coleridge's house is the most prominent one, so I'll make that our first heading."

"Have you talked to Myles recently?" Jon asked casually.

"Why, yes. Just a little while ago. I have a painting in the gallery he's shown some interest in."

"He's in Nantucket then?"

"Why shouldn't he be?" She seemed vaguely annoyed by the question.

Jon shrugged. "I heard he was traveling a lot on business. I didn't expect him to be here."

"Maybe he had business on Nantucket," Ariel suggested.

"Maybe so."

"Did Lorelei come with you on this trip?" she asked, changing the subject.

"No."

"When did you arrive?"

"This morning."

"Really?" she asked. "And how long will you be staying?"

"I hope to take the six o'clock plane back."

Her eyebrows rose. "You mean today?"

"That's right."

"My gracious, Jon. That's a long distance to travel for a one-day visit. What pleasures of the island will you enjoy in so short a time?"

"I came because I hoped you and I could talk."

She looked out at the water, as if not hearing what he'd said. "I think I'll come about to port. Put your head down before the sail swings, and move over to the other side."

She pulled the tiller toward her, and Jon crouched as the boom of the sail swung to the port side. At the same time, he shifted his position and sat along the starboard deck to balance the boat. Ariel, meanwhile, busied herself adjusting the angle of the sail and checking the wind direction from the telltale of red ribbon fluttering at the top of the mast.

"Now, wasn't I right?" she asked after a moment. "Isn't it more pleasant out here on the water?"

"Very."

"By the way, I call my boat the *Oracle,*" she said. "Like me, she has a sense of what the future holds. Do you know what the future holds, Jon?"

He shook his head. "I can't say that I do."

She smiled. "So I guess I have an advantage over you. Now tell me, Jon, why did you come all this way to talk with me?"

Once more, his instinct told him: Proceed cautiously. Be careful.

"As you know," he began, "I think a lot of Brian. He's a good man. With a good heart."

"He's the best," Ariel agreed. "I'm very lucky."

"And you know he and I are very close as friends."

"I do indeed. In fact, you were at his house last night. He told me that."

"I was," Jon said. "I brought him up to date on what I've learned so far."

"Learned about what, Jon?"

"For one thing, about the person who killed Abel Lasher."

"Really?"

"And who forged the Audubon Quartet."

"They're the same person?"

"Yes."

"Goodness me, you have been busy, Jon. And may I ask who this 'person' is?"

"Jack Briscoe," he said simply.

Ariel drew in a little breath, then looked out at the harbor.

"Jack . . . Jack . . . poor sad old Jack," she said at last. "I'm shocked to even think he could be capable of such a thing." She added, "But I'm not surprised."

"May I ask why not?"

Her face became a portrait of sad sympathy. "Because I've always thought of Jack as—how shall I describe him?—as an unstable character. It probably goes back to his childhood. His parents were both killed in the war. The violence he must have seen. The deaths."

"I also think he murdered that young model in New York," Jon said.

"*Two* murders! Gracious! We ought to call him Jack the Ripper." Ariel McKenzie laughed, a mocking laugh that had the sound of someone walking over broken glass. "Why would he do such a thing?"

"Because the girl knew about the Lasher murder and the forgeries. She was modeling for other artists, but she lived with Jack. She was into drugs and wanted out; she wanted to buy back her life. She needed money, and the way to get a lot of it was by exposing Jack."

"But if Jack did all these horrible things, why didn't the police arrest him?"

"Because they couldn't find him," Jon said. "He went into hiding after she was killed."

"Then if you knew all this, why didn't *you* go to the police yourself?"

"Because I thought I could also connect him to the forged Audubons."

She shook her head. "Well, I've known Jack for a few years as an artist, but I can't believe he'd stoop to forgery."

"The fact is, he's done art forgery much of his career . . . under another name."

"And what would that name be?" she inquired.

"Jeremy Breen."

The sailboat lurched sideways. Ariel stood suddenly and looked down over the side. "Oh, dear—I've been careless. We're in shallow water, Jon."

She sat down again and pulled the tiller. Instantly, the sail swung in Jon's direction. He ducked as the heavy boom swept just above his head. When he was seated on the other side of the boat, he noticed they were well out in the harbor.

"Please, do go on, Jon," Ariel suggested as the boat began to gather speed again. "How could Jack have forged the Audubons? Brian kept them in his house in Boston under lock and key."

"I wondered the same thing," Jon said, "since Brian swore the paintings had been guarded on the trip from Boston to Nantucket. That meant the real watercolors had been switched with forgeries before they left his house."

"By whom?"

"One of the three people who had access to the house with any regularity—Brian himself, Mrs. Ferris . . . and you."

Behind the sunglasses, Ariel regarded him. Her face showed no alarm; rather, there was an expression of concern, as if he had been talking about someone neither of them really knew.

"Did you tell all this to Brian?" she asked.

"No. But someone has to," Jon said. "And that person should be you."

Ariel glanced up at the ribbon on the masthead, which was snapping briskly now. "The wind is coming up," she said. Again she looked at Jon. "What else do you know?"

"I know Jeremy Breen went to prison for trying to sell some fake Picasso drawings to a Boston gallery owner named Pantelli." He paused. "I also know Breen had an accomplice—a young woman who was working in the gallery."

"Fascinating."

" 'Brunch on Boston Common,' " Jon said. "Does that mean something to you?"

Ariel was silent, but the muscles of her jaw grew tight.

"It was a parody of Manet's 'Luncheon on the Grass,' " Jon continued. "The figures in the painting were the three assistants Pantelli employed in his gallery. I saw the painting yesterday."

"Then you know I was that woman."

"Yes."

"Pantelli was an odious little man," Ariel said. "I'm sorry Jeremy didn't kill him when he had the chance. He probably would have if the two had been alone."

She made a slight adjustment in the sail. As she spoke, she watched it fill with wind and billow forward, giving the boat even greater speed.

"I met Jeremy the year I started working at the gallery," she continued, not looking at Jon. "We became lovers. He was a very charismatic man; anything he asked of me, I'd do. He thought Pantelli was an easy mark, and after their first meeting, he thought he could sell the Picasso drawings to him with no questions asked. Then I found out Pantelli was suspicious. I urged Jeremy not to go back to the gallery, but he insisted. He was sure Pantelli would accept the drawings, even if he thought they weren't the real thing."

The sail began flapping noisily. Her eyes darted to it, as did Jon's. She drew in the sail and the flapping stopped. But now Jon was looking at the sky. The clouds had lowered and become thick enough to hide the sun. Ariel removed her sunglasses, folded them and placed them in the carryall, next to her feet.

"After Breen's release from prison," Jon asked, "did the two of you get back together?"

Her eyes studied him before she answered. "Yes. At first we

corresponded off and on. I'd gone to New York. Jeremy followed me. He changed his name and grew a beard. But otherwise, he was the same, the man I'd loved. And he returned to painting—some of his own things, but also forgeries he knew would sell. Picasso, Braque, Dufy."

"How did he market them?"

"Through a collector he had met. Then, three years ago, he offered some for sale to an art dealer in SoHo. That was a mistake."

"What do you mean?"

"The dealer was dubious about a fake Cezanne that Jeremy—or Jack, as he wanted me to call him—had for sale. We decided New York might become, in Jack's words, 'much too hot.' So we moved back to Boston."

"When did you meet Brian?"

"Earlier this year. In March. We met at a party on Nantucket. He asked me what I did and I told him I was interested in art. The next thing I knew, he bought the Wide Wharf Gallery and gave it to me as a gift. Soon after that, he asked me to become his wife, and I said yes. I loved him. I still do."

"And Jack?"

"By then, it was over with us. He'd found other women—models who posed for him, mostly. But we stayed friends."

"Enough to substitute the real Audubons with the copies Briscoe made of them?"

"Yes."

"But, Brian?"

"How could I deceive him if I loved him?" she asked, turning to Jon now. "Jack convinced me that Brian wouldn't know the difference. Jack needed money and someone he knew offered him a great deal of it for the real Audubons."

Ariel gave a dismissive shrug. "The plan would have worked, too, if Abel Lasher hadn't spotted the copies at the reception."

"So Jack decided he would murder Lasher," Jon said. "Rather than returning to his beach house, Briscoe followed Lasher to the ferry, found him on the deck, and strangled him."

"Yes. He was sure that when Lasher revealed the forgeries, it was only the beginning. He was sure that if Lasher lived, he'd use his magazine to print an exposé about them and an investigation would begin. Jack couldn't let that happen."

"When did Jack tell you all that?" he asked.

"After the reception ended. Jack was furious. I also know he can be a violent person. I was afraid of what he might do. So I went with him on the boat to beg him not to."

"You were on the ferry that night?"

"Yes. I stayed inside the Jeep. With its dark windows, nobody could see in. I pleaded with Jack not to do anything to Lasher. But Jack said that if he was discovered as the forger, he'd go back to prison. Prison had been awful for him. Terrible. He said he'd rather die than go back there."

Momentarily, the wind blew her dark hair against her face. She brushed it back. "He found Lasher on deck, used a piece of picture cord to strangle him, and threw the body overboard. After the ferry reached Hyannis, Jack and I spent the night at a motel near the marina. The next morning, Jack drove to New York and I took the early ferry back.

"It was the same thing with the girl. She was living with him," Ariel went on. "I'd told him you were pursuing several people who might have been involved in Lasher's murder. Jack was one. When he found out the girl had contacted you and was about to identify him as the murderer, he killed her."

"After that, he came directly to Nantucket, didn't he?" Jon asked.

"Yes."

"To your house on Hussey Street. Is he there now?"

"Yes." To Jon's surprise, tears began to fill her eyes. "He's there now," Ariel confirmed. "He's dead."

"Dead?"

"When he was asleep, I strangled him the way he did the others. With a picture cord. There was so much I wanted, so many things I was about to have—a wonderful new life, marriage to the man I loved. Jack could have ruined everything."

She raised her head. When she spoke again, her voice had a distant, dreamlike quality. "I had to kill him. Do you see?"

"I see," he told her, with a sympathy and sorrow that were genuine.

Then, looking past her, Jon realized they were approaching the enormous granite rocks that made up the twin jetties at the harbor entrance.

"Ariel, we're heading for deep water," he cautioned. "Turn the boat around."

Instead, with her free hand she picked up the carryall and placed it on her lap. "Do you know what's in this bag, Jon?"

"No."

"My life. Letters, papers, documents, the love letters Jack wrote to me from prison. Some are very beautiful. Now no one will ever know how beautiful they were."

Abruptly, Ariel stood, keeping one hand on the tiller. In a sweeping gesture with the other hand, she flung the carryall into the sea. The bag sank, disappearing in an instant as a wave rolled over it.

"Ariel, sit down," Jon told her quietly.

She sat and smiled at him like a child waiting to be complimented for a good deed done.

"Ariel . . . listen to me, please."

"The wind is picking up, Jon. Do you feel it?"

"Yes. Listen . . . where are the Audubons? Who has them? I think I know. Tell me."

" 'The birds of the air shall tell you,' " she responded, waving vaguely at the gulls circling overhead against an angry sky.

"That's from the Bible, Jon. Did you know that? My father always read the Bible to me when I was a child. Maybe the birds of the air can tell you where the Audubons have flown."

She threw the tiller to the side. The sail swept above Jon just as he ducked to the cockpit deck. Emerging on the other side of the boat, he was alarmed now at the parade of vessels—cruisers, sailboats, fishing boats, all headed in the opposite direction, hurrying for port.

Suddenly the reason for their haste was chillingly apparent. Looking west, Jon saw the sky was black, fractured by sharp streaks of lightning. Below it was a roiling, angry sea.

"There's a storm coming!" he shouted.

"Yes!" Ariel shouted back. "Feel it! Feel the wind, Jon! Isn't it wonderful!"

She laughed a wild, insane laugh.

A wave smashed over the bow, cascading down into the open boat, drenching them. Ariel's hands gripped the tiller with such force they were a bloodless white.

"For God's sake, Ariel!" he told her. "We're sailing into a storm! You're going to kill us both!"

Jon couldn't hear her answer, but he could read it on her lips: "I know."

The bow of the boat lifted, hung cantilevered in space for

several seconds, then slammed down with jolting force. A cross wind spun the boat, pitching her at a sharp angle before plummeting her headfirst into a trough between two mounting waves. Head back, Ariel regarded them with a look of beatific wonder on her face.

The rain began now, huge drops that stung the skin like beebee shot. Turning, Jon saw they were well into Nantucket Sound. He had a fleeting vision of the shore, of a bluff on which a line of stately houses stood. A moment later, they too disappeared behind the sheets of windswept rain.

Jon braced his feet against the gunwale opposite. With both hands, he gripped the mast. If he'd had any hope of taking control of the boat from Ariel, it was too late.

Ahead, the sea was an expanse of tumbling white foam. Above them, gray-green clouds, pendulant and ominous, sped toward them. Lightning flashed everywhere around them. Thunder roared above the raging wind.

The boat rolled violently, one instant airborne, then flung downward into space.

There was a wrenching, splintering of wood. The cleat that held the sail line tore free. Instantly, the sail whipped out, twisted crazily, began to shred. Jon heard sharp pinging sounds: the snapping of the wire shrouds that held the mast.

Plunged into another trough, the boat spun, foundered, listing as the waves on either side grew higher.

It was the moment Ariel McKenzie had been waiting for. She let go of the tiller and stood up. Eyes closed, head back, she let out a cry of anguish and despair—and threw herself into the sea.

The next moment, the sailboat capsized.

DARKNESS. COLD. SWIRLING water tearing at his limbs.

Swim! Kick! Jon told himself. Look for the surface. Find the triangle of white sail. Struggle upward. Swim.

His lungs fought desperately for air. Above him, he saw the overturned hull of the boat, separated from the broken mast. He forced his hands to reach for it. He missed, and lunged again.

Finally, as he struck the surface of the water, an object slammed against his back. He turned and saw it was the wooden rudder, which had torn loose from the hull.

He clung to it and floated, choking, coughing, gasping for his life, for air. Then, gripping the sides of the rudder, he hoisted his body onto it. He lay on it, letting himself be carried upward by a wave.

Around him, he heard the tumult of the wind and waves. But gradually he heard another sound—a deep and steady roar. He raised his head to look in its direction. What he saw filled him with both hope and dread.

A hundred yards ahead, there was a narrow beach below a bluff. A canopy of frothy foam stretched out from it, lifting and falling with the curling of each wave that approached. One after another, in thunderous succession, the waves crashed down onto the sloping sand.

Jon knew it was his only chance. Pushing hard against the tide, he turned the rudder toward the beach and paddled with all the strength left in him.

The closer he came to the beach, the more deafening the noise of the surf became. Fifty yards from it, he felt the rudder rise. Veils of spume, airborne by the wind, momentarily blinded him.

He kept on.

Forty yards.

Then thirty.

Twenty.

Ten.

The wave rose toward a crest, lifted, lifted—and began to curl. . . .

Now!

Jon flung himself into the water. Spun onto his back, he saw the breaking wave arc over him. An instant later, it smashed onto the beach, carrying him with it.

Fingers digging into the wet sand, he struggled forward in the uprush, fighting to hold on. He felt the seaward pull of the retreating water clutch at him. He pressed his body against the sand, desperate to resist the undertow.

Another wave crashed down on him with truncheon force. As it withdrew, he paused to catch his breath, and crawled again in the direction of the bluff.

His body throbbed with pain. His ears rang. His skin was raw from the rough sand.

But he was alive.

Jon closed his eyes and said a grateful prayer for that.

Then he passed out.

PRODDING. A SHARP object pressed into his back. Jon groaned.

"You're alive at least," a voice said. "I was afraid—let me say, I wasn't sure . . ."

Jon opened his eyes. He remained facedown, but turned his head and saw that he was staring at the tips of two black Wellington boots. Beside them was a walking stick.

"Excuse me if I poked you with my stick," the voice went on, "but I thought you might be dead."

Jon rolled to his side and looked up. Above him stood a short, elderly man in a double-breasted navy blazer and a yachting cap.

"Good Lord—Mr. Wilder!" the man exclaimed. "We met on the Nantucket ferry. I'm Thomas Swain. I thought I saw a sailboat out there in the storm. Was that you?"

Jon nodded yes, then coughed.

"I live in a house up on the bluff," Swain said. "Stay here. I'll go back and call the hospital and the police. I'll also ask my wife to get a blanket and put coffee in a thermos. I suspect you're rather chilled."

"Thanks. Coffee would be good." Jon struggled to sit up.

"Be careful now. Don't strain." Commodore Swain paused. There was a look of mild disapproval on his face. "Uh, Mr. Wilder, it's not the most propitious moment to say this, but on the ferry when we spoke, you said you'd done some sailing. You know the first lesson a sailor learns is to seek shelter in a storm. It was foolhardy of you, my young friend, to try to ride it out, as you appeared to do. You could have gotten yourself killed."

"I know," was all Jon said.

"A word to the wise," Swain concluded and started for a set of wooden steps that led up the bluff.

Jon turned his head and looked in the direction of the water. The storm's intensity had passed. The sky was filled now with swift-moving clouds that parted briefly to let shafts of sunlight through. Along the water's edge, the surf still pounded, but with a comforting familiarity.

Close to the water, just beyond the shoreline, seabirds skimmed the waves. Farther out, whitecaps were still visible.

But for the most part, the surface appeared ingenuously peaceful, undulating with broad, rolling swells.

Yet as Jon gazed out at the vast expanse, there was no sign of Ariel McKenzie's boat—no hull, no broken mast, not even the rudder that had saved Jon's life.

As it had done with Ariel and her dark secrets, the sea had taken everything and left no trace.

19

THE DESK CLERK smiled. "I hope you enjoyed your visit to Nantucket, Mr. Wilder."

Jon took his credit card and the receipt she handed him. "It was an experience," he answered pleasantly.

"I'm afraid, though, that with the fog, the flights have been backed up. You may have to wait a while at the airport."

"I don't mind. Do you know if someone called a taxi?"

"Yes, sir. It should be here very soon."

"Thank you."

He walked across the lobby of the Jared Coffin House and sat down in a leather wing chair. Built as the home of a Nantucket shipowner in the mid-nineteenth century, the beautiful old inn had been restored to its historic elegance.

Jon relaxed into the comfort of the chair and thought back to what had transpired yesterday. Much of it he wished he could forget. After arriving at the beach below Swain's house, the emergency medical unit had transported him to the Nantucket hospital and he had been given a complete examination. Except for hypothermia and fatigue, he was found to be in good physical condition. He was released several hours later with the admonition not to travel for a day or so, and to rest. Commodore Swain had offered him the opportunity of staying in his home overnight. When Jon declined, Swain suggested getting him a room at the Jared Coffin House. Generally, the inn was fully booked, but Swain had somehow managed to secure a reservation. The Swains and Coffins were among Nantucket's first settlers, the Commodore had told Jon, and that counted for something.

After arriving at the inn, he'd called Lorelei to tell her he was on Nantucket—"checking on a few details," were his words—and he assured her he would return to Scarborough the next day. In spite of her persistent questions, he mentioned nothing of what had occurred that afternoon.

Then he had put in a call to Brian Ravener.

As Jon learned, the Nantucket police had already informed Ravener of Ariel McKenzie's death. Her body had been discovered about seven in the evening yesterday, washed up on a lonely stretch of beach along Coskata. To Jon's regret, they'd also told Ravener that the body of Jack Briscoe had been discovered strangled in the house on Hussey Street. Jon had given the police the information, but he wished afterward he could have been the one to tell his friend.

When John had talked with Ravener himself, the man was still grief-stricken and unwilling to believe Ariel's involvement in the crimes. Jon was certain nonetheless that given time, he would come to understand and to accept the truth. Perhaps when Ravener looked back, his sorrow would be made less bitter by recollections of the truly loving moments he and Ariel had shared.

After completing his calls, Jon had ordered a light supper in the room, then crawled under the covers of the canopied four-poster bed and gone to sleep. He had slept heavily and dreamlessly, waking at ten this morning, far later than was usual for him. Swain had also seen to it that he was provided with some toiletries and a change of clothes. Arising, Jon had taken a luxurious hot bath, shaved, dressed, had breakfast again in his room, and requested that a taxi fetch him at eleven thirty to transport him to the airport.

Looking at the lobby clock, Jon saw it was eleven thirty now. Rather than remain there, he decided he would wait outside. He rose and headed to the doors. He opened them and discovered that a good deal of the morning fog had burned away.

He checked the traffic along Broad Street, then started down the stone steps of the inn. As he reached the sidewalk, he noticed a green Jaguar XJ6 sitting at the curb. The driver saw Jon and stepped out.

It was Myles Coleridge.

As he came forward, he gave Jon a hearty wave. "Good morning," Coleridge called.

"Hello, Myles."

"What luck that you're still here."

Coleridge was dressed in the same white outfit Jon remembered from the visit to The Aerie: white shirt and breeches, along with black boots. A lightweight brown aviator jacket, partially unzipped, was worn over the shirt.

He grasped Jon's hand and shook it. "I heard the news last night. Just terrible. I also called Brian to offer my condolences. I said that whatever I could do to help, I would."

"How thoughtful." Jon withdrew his hand.

"Brian told me you were staying here and that you planned to take a noon flight to Hyannis. That's when I knew exactly what to do."

"Oh? What would that be?"

"Drive you to the airport."

"That won't be necessary," Jon said.

"But I want to," Coleridge insisted.

"Myles, I have a taxi coming any minute."

"I sent it away."

"What?"

"When I arrived, I saw the fellow waiting at the curb. I told him that I was a friend of yours and I was here to pick you up."

Jon realized that as Coleridge had been speaking, he had continually edged closer, so that now Jon's back was against one of the stone newel posts at the bottom of the steps.

"What's more," Coleridge continued, "I'd be pleased to fly you to Hyannis in my plane. I was planning to fly to Boston today anyway and I can drop you on the way. Do you have anything to bring?"

"No. Look, Myles—"

"Good." Coleridge offered a thin smile. "Then why don't you and I get into my car?"

"I don't want to do that, Myles."

"I suggest you get into the car, Jon." It was an order. "Now."

Jon saw Coleridge's right hand reach into the pocket of the aviator jacket. At the base, the pocket pointed outward, as if from a protruding finger—or a spotting scope. Jon knew it was neither.

Coleridge kept his voice low, but conversational. "Jon, I don't wish to make this disagreeable. I'm sure you know what's in my pocket."

"Yes."

"Therefore, you will accompany me, as I request. At the airport, I'll park in the long-term lot. From there, you and I will walk together to the terminal, through it, and out into the runway apron where the planes are parked. Mine will be among them."

"Myles, this is stupid."

"It would be more stupid not to follow my instructions, Jon. Get into the car."

With Coleridge at his side, Jon walked around to the passenger side of the Jaguar and climbed in. Moments later, Coleridge slid in behind the wheel. Jon heard a click. The doors were locked.

The engine roared to life and Coleridge pulled out from the curb.

THEY ROUNDED THE rotary and turned onto the airport road. Soon Jon saw two large hangars. Beyond them was the airport entrance, leading to the parking lot and terminal.

Coleridge slowed at the entrance, drove into the long-term lot and found a spot. He turned off the motor.

"Let's go," he said. They were the first words he'd spoken since they'd left the inn. "When I unlock the doors, step out and stand facing the car."

Jon heard the door locks disengage. He stepped out and stood beside the Jaguar as Coleridge had instructed.

"Very good, Jon," Coleridge murmured as he joined him. "Now walk slightly ahead of me and to my right. As we enter the terminal, ignore the two policemen."

Jon did as he was told.

They continued through the main entrance of the terminal. Despite the air conditioning inside, Jon felt perspiration clinging to his shirt.

"Keep going," Coleridge urged.

The lobby of the terminal itself was thronged with people—passengers from recently arriving flights, others waiting to depart, families at the snack bar, scores of tourists pouring over postcards and Nantucket trinkets at the shops.

The two men walked together toward the area reserved for passengers waiting to board flights. Ahead, airport security personnel were shepherding people single file through the metal-detection frame. The sight of it gave Jon momentary hope.

Instead, as they reached the checkpoint, Coleridge flashed a badge to the guards, made an abrupt right turn and started toward a set of double doors. Beyond them was the apron of the runway, where several private planes were parked.

Among them was a white twin-engine Piper Navajo. A thin red stripe ran lengthwise along the fuselage. Near the tail, Jon could see the registration number of the aircraft: N264YB. A ground-service mechanic in gray overalls stood behind one of the stabilizers, testing the action of the flap. He noticed Jon and Coleridge coming toward him and waved. Coleridge then did a quick pre-flight check.

"The plane's ready," Coleridge said to Jon, no longer whispering. "We can go."

Jon's pulse began to race. He felt Coleridge pressing at his side. There were other people in the area, but they became a blur. Jon continued toward the plane.

"Excuse me," a man said suddenly. He stood directly in Jon's path. The man was dressed in shorts and a T-shirt that bore the initials "CAS" across the front.

Jon halted. Coleridge did the same.

With the man were several other men and women, wearing T-shirts similar to his. "Excuse me," the man repeated, "but are you Jon Wilder?"

Jon hesitated. "Yes."

"What's going on here?" Coleridge demanded testily.

"We're with the Cincinnati Audubon Society," the man explained. He turned to Jon again. "It's an honor to meet you, Mr. Wilder. We're using your 'Guide to Eastern Shorebirds' on this trip. I recognized you from the photo in the book."

"Oh, for Chrissake," Coleridge hissed into Jon's ear. "Get rid of these people."

A young woman thrust a nature guide and a pen in Jon's direction. "Here's my copy, Mr. Wilder," she piped. "Would you sign it, please?"

Jon glanced at Coleridge.

"All right, all right—sign it," Coleridge snapped. He peered over Jon's shoulder, watching what Jon wrote.

Jon took the book and signed it quickly. Immediately, copies were spread open around him by the other members of the group.

Another young woman tugged at Coleridge's jacket sleeve. "Are you a birder, too?" she asked.

He whirled on her. "No! Leave us alone!"

Startled, the group backed away. Coleridge shoved Jon forward. They continued to the plane.

Reaching it, Coleridge leaned over the right wing beside the fuselage and opened the cabin door.

"Get in," he ordered.

Jon boosted himself onto the wing and swung around into the cabin, taking the right-hand seat. Coleridge slammed the cabin door and locked it. Several moments later, he appeared at the left wing. He opened the door and climbed into the pilot's seat. He rammed in his seatbelt, put on dark aviator glasses, and secured the earphone with a microphone attachment to his head.

He started the engines, flipped a variety of switches, scanned the instrument panel hurriedly, then tested the control yoke and pedals. Finally, he spoke into the microphone: "Two-six-four-Yankee-Bravo. Request permission to taxi to the active."

Coleridge waited. Suddenly, surprise swept across his face. "What do you mean, hold? Hold for what?"

He leaned forward, looking left and right, then up. "Say again—hold for *what?* No one's on the runway or on final!"

His face flushed, and small beads of sweat were blossoming on his bald head.

He glanced left again, then slid back the window panel. Looking also, Jon could see the ground mechanic running toward the plane.

"What's wrong?" Coleridge shouted as the man approached the wing.

"Sorry, sir," the mechanic called. "But the rotating beacon on the tail isn't working."

"Of course it's working," Coleridge flared. "Two days ago I had the plane inspected. It was working then."

"The tower said it isn't now, sir," the mechanic told him. "Try the switch again."

The mechanic moved away from the wing and looked back toward the tail of the plane. Meanwhile, Coleridge manipulated a control-panel switch impatiently.

"Okay!" the mechanic called. "It seems to be okay. But turn it off and on a few more times to make sure."

Coleridge hurled an obscenity at the mechanic and slammed the window panel shut. He tore the earphone from his head and threw it down. Out of the earpiece, the voice of the tower operator could be heard, still ordering the plane to hold.

Instead, Coleridge shoved the throttles forward, spun the airplane onto the taxiway and began racing toward the south end of the field, the plane rocking as it sped.

Faintly, in the distance, sirens sounded.

The airplane whipped onto the approach marks, pivoting again onto the runway. Jon was slammed back in his seat as Coleridge pushed the throttles to full power. Instantly, the plane sought take-off speed.

Then, at the far end of the runway, they appeared—two Nantucket police cars dashing toward them with their roof lights flashing, sirens blistering the air.

Abruptly, a third car drove onto the runway directly in the plane's path, blocking it from taking off.

Instinctively, Coleridge jammed down on the brakes. The plane fishtailed, spun around, then skidded to a screaming halt and slid onto the grass.

Coleridge whirled at Jon. "Damn you!"

Jon saw a fourth police car racing down the taxiway toward them.

"It's over, Myles. Give it up," he said. "It was your idea, wasn't it, for Jack Briscoe to steal the Audubon Quartet with Ariel's help and to replace them with forgeries?"

"You have no proof of that."

"Except that you and Briscoe talked a great deal in the

weeks leading up to the reception. His telephone bill shows calls to New York State. My guess is it's your number at The Aerie. He also wrote it on a pad beside his telephone, along with what is probably the number of your Nantucket house."

"We talked, yes," Coleridge said, "but it was about some of Briscoe's newer paintings. I wanted to buy them."

"Including the forged Winslow Homer you showed Lorelei and me the night we visited you?"

Coleridge turned his head away. From the airport service buildings near the tower, a yellow rescue truck was coming fast.

"I mailed the bill and the piece of paper with your telephone numbers to the police," continued Jon, "along with a short note. I also told them they might want a tour of your art collection. All of it, including the Audubon Quartet."

Coleridge remained silent, watching as the police cars began encircling the plane. Officers leaped out and crouched behind their vehicles, weapons drawn.

"It's over, Myles," Jon repeated. "The police are waiting for you to get out of the plane."

It was as if the man had never heard him. Rather, he continued staring out the window of the cabin, watching the increasing number of police officers, including one who was readying a bullhorn.

Finally, Myles Coleridge leaned back against his seat and closed his eyes. A few moments later, he opened them, unfastened his seatbelt, pushed open the door, and stepped out onto the wing with his hands raised.

20

THEY WERE MAGNIFICENT.

Displayed on the long table in Brian Ravener's dining room, the four Audubon watercolors were even more superb than Jon could have envisioned.

All were just as Audubon himself had painted them: on watercolor paper of the finest quality and without frames. Remarkably, they showed little sign of age. The paint itself maintained a luster that was startling—the vivid-yellow wing bars of the goldfinch, the black-and-white harlequin face of the Montezuma quail, the subtle gray-brown of the sage sparrow, the speckled chest and blazing dark eyes of the spotted owl.

"Behold the *real* Audubon Quartet," Ravener said. The statement was self-evident; seeing the authentic Audubons spread out before them now, the difference between these and the forgeries was obvious.

"They're wonderful," Jon said.

"Apparently the police obtained a search warrant to The Aerie the day of Coleridge's arrest. They found them in a room with other paintings Coleridge kept well hidden."

Ravener moved a hand over the paintings in a proprietary gesture. "It took a few days to work out their return, but I received them late last week."

"And they went straight into your vault, I'm sure."

"You bet they did. I wouldn't even show them to the media," Ravener said. "The newspapers and TV people wanted a big story, given Coleridge's involvement and the paintings' value. But I won't let the originals be photographed. You're the first person to see them, except for the police."

"I'm honored."

Ravener put an arm around Jon's shoulders. "It's the least I could do, considering you nearly lost your life to get them back. How are you feeling, by the way?"

"Better," Jon answered. "But I don't know how long it'll be before I can step into a sailboat or airplane again."

He paused, then added, "How about you?"

The other gave an offhand wave. But there was sadness in his eyes. "I'm better, too, I suppose," Ravener said. "It's taken me a while, though. In the beginning, it was rough."

"I'm sure."

"They found most of Ariel's boat, you know. As for the letters and whatever she threw overboard, they're gone, disappeared. It's probably just as well."

"Have you been back to Nantucket?" Jon inquired.

"No. The woman who was Ariel's gallery assistant identified the body. And Ariel's brother made arrangements for her to be buried in the family plot outside Savannah. Chapter closed.

"So, now . . ." Ravener went on, "let me tell you about tomorrow's ceremony."

"Yes. I'd like to hear about it."

"First, we'll have lunch at the Museum of Fine Arts at one,

in the trustees' dining room. The ceremony is at three. The director will say something appropriate, as will a few others from the arts community, and then I'll make my presentation of the Audubons to the museum."

"It's a very generous donation."

"The paintings deserve to be seen by a lot more people than me and a few friends," Ravener said. "I'm going to keep Audubon's letter, though. It's a fascinating glimpse into a part of the man's life that no one knew about."

"You also mentioned dinner here tomorrow night."

"Yes," Ravener confirmed. "I've asked Dr. La Tour and his wife. It'll be just the six of us."

"Six?"

"Ah—a slip of the tongue." The man allowed a smile. "I've invited a mystery guest, too."

"Anyone I know?"

Ravener held up a hand. "I say no more. Look, why don't you go down to the garden? I'll put these paintings in the vault, then fix us drinks."

Conversation drifted from the direction of the kitchen. Ravener inclined his head. "Lorelei can keep you company, if I can pry her away from the loquacious Mrs. Ferris."

He took Jon's arm and guided him toward the rear portion of the house, and finally to a door. Beyond it was a set of steps that led down into a small garden that made up a section of the courtyard.

Descending the steps, Jon found himself on a stone terrace under a leafy pergola. He sought out a comfortably cushioned garden chair and eased into it. From the terrace, several paths meandered out into the garden, past small statuary and a fountain from which water softly splashed. The waning sunlight of the summer evening touched only the roofs and chimneys of the surrounding buildings, filling the garden and the courtyard with a shadowed golden glow.

The door at the top of the steps opened and Ravener appeared, carrying a gin-and-tonic in each hand. He joined Jon, handed him a glass, then sat down on a stone bench facing him.

"To long life," Ravener toasted, raising his glass. "And I apologize again for jeopardizing yours on my behalf. If I'd known all the dangers you'd have faced, I never would have asked you for your help."

"It was my own fault for getting into the sailboat with Ariel," admitted Jon. "I hoped I could convince her to go to the police. I thought—wrongly, as it turned out—that I could reason with her."

Ravener gave a slow shake of the head. "By then, she was beyond reason, I suspect."

Jon nodded. "I'm afraid she was."

"Of course, you didn't volunteer to go with Coleridge."

"No. And Coleridge knew it. The gun was part of his unfriendly persuasion to force me to go with him."

"But once the two of you were in his plane . . ." He grimaced. "What do you suppose Coleridge had in mind?"

"Who knows? When he approached me outside the Jared Coffin House, he told me he'd be pleased to drop me off enroute. He might have meant it literally."

"I heard the police found two bullets in the chamber of his gun. Maybe he meant to kill you and himself and crash the plane."

This time it was Jon who grimaced. "Maybe. But that's speculation, too. The man isn't talking, even to his lawyer."

"You never told me how you stopped Coleridge and his plane from taking off."

"The Cincinnati bird group gets the real credit," Jon said.

"What do you mean?"

"As Coleridge and I were walking toward his plane, some birders interrupted us. They happened to be carrying my nature guide, recognized me, and asked if I would autograph their books. Because we were together, they thought Coleridge was a birder also. When a woman temporarily distracted him, I wrote in the book I was signing 'STOP N264YB'—the registration numbers on Coleridge's plane."

"So the light on the plane's tail wasn't really broken?"

"No. That was a stall the tower operator used to give the police time to get there."

"But what made you suspicious of Coleridge in the first place?"

"Several things," Jon said. "At the presentation of the Audubons on the night of the reception, you misidentified the small animal the spotted owl had just killed. You said it was a mole. But when Ariel and I visited Coleridge's estate, he mentioned—correctly, as it happened—that the rodent was a vole. During the unveiling of the paintings, he and Meredith were standing at the far side of the room near us. From that distance, he couldn't possibly have noted the distinction."

"And what else?"

"On that same visit, Coleridge showed us a seascape called 'Safe Harbor.' He said it had been done by Winslow Homer. The fact is, I'd seen the painting, or probably a copy of it, in the truck Jack Briscoe was driving when he showed up at the Kreutzer Museum the day I was there.

"Finally, on that visit to Briscoe's beach house, I found several telephone numbers I guessed might belong to Coleridge. The out-of-state calls on the bill in Briscoe's mailbox matched Coleridge's private number at The Aerie. According to the bill, Briscoe had called Coleridge frequently in the month before the reception. That's when I was sure Coleridge was behind the scheme. He also knew I suspected him and maybe thought I had more evidence against him. That's why he came after me."

Ravener grunted. "So Duncan Rutledge was right when he said a member of The Collectors' Club probably had the real Audubons. That would include Coleridge."

"When Rutledge and I talked," Jon recalled, "he mentioned that there were a few names in particular he'd give me after the auction. As it was, he died before he had the chance."

"But about the real paintings," Ravener asked, "how did Briscoe get access to them so he could forge them?"

"He depended on Ariel. Although you kept the originals locked in your vault, you must have left them unsecured for a period of time when she was in your house."

"I did", admitted Ravener. "Once I let her have them for several days while I was gone. She said she wanted to think about how the paintings should be framed."

"During which she either photographed them," Jon said, "and gave them to Briscoe, or allowed him into the house to copy them. She also repeated to Briscoe everything you told her about my investigation. And he passed it along to Coleridge."

"Was she . . . was Ariel so much in love with Briscoe?" Ravener asked after a moment.

"She was once, maybe. Years ago. It ended. But he still held a certain power over her."

"And now both Ariel and Jack Briscoe are dead, along with the young model. All because of Coleridge's arrogance and greed." Ravener stood, his disgust visible.

Somewhere in the house, a telephone began to ring. The door at the top of the steps opened and Lorelei appeared.

"Brian, someone on the phone would like to speak with you," she called.

Ravener excused himself and headed up the steps.

As he disappeared into the house, Lorelei came down to the courtyard and took the bench Ravener had vacated. "Mrs. Ferris prepared hors d'oeuvres," she told Jon. "I'll get you some, if you like."

"Yes. Thanks."

From within the house, they heard Ravener's voice on the telephone, followed by a laugh.

Jon glanced toward the sound. "That's the first time I've heard Brian really laugh since the whole business of the Audubons began."

"I'm not sure who called him," Lorelei said, "but I suspect it may be Meredith Coleridge."

"Which makes *me* suspect who tomorrow night's mystery dinner guest will be."

Lorelei looked pleased. "That would be nice."

Suddenly she rose. "I just remembered I promised you hors d'oeuvres. I'll be right back."

She left and hurried up the steps to the house.

Alone again, Jon leaned back, letting the serenity and beauty of the twilit garden weave their graceful spell.

Yet, as he listened, he discovered it was not so quiet after all. Everywhere around him, garden birds were chattering. On a feeder, chickadees and a variety of finches bickered over seeds;

in berry bushes near the fountain, catbirds darted, mewing their familiar call.

Watching the birds, he was reminded once more of the brilliant watercolor paintings John James Audubon had made of them: the catbirds feasting on lush blackberries, the purple finches poised delicately on pine boughs, chickadees perched on a willow oak.

As an artist and a naturalist, Audubon had had no peer. He was a genius, that was sure. For Jon himself, beginning with the moment he first sketched an outline of a bird on watercolor paper, Audubon had been his inspiration, mentor, guide.

"Still, Mr. Audubon," Jon said aloud, "if you'd stayed home in 1843 instead of going west, you would have made my life a whole lot easier."

He heard a sound behind him. Turning, he saw Lorelei standing at the bottom of the steps, a small tray in her hand.

"I brought you some hors d'oeuvres," she said.

She came to him and handed him the tray, but remained standing, studying him somewhat quizzically.

"Excuse me for asking," she went on, "but as I was coming down the steps, I thought I heard you talking to someone."

"Actually, I was."

"Who?"

Jon gave her a wry smile.

"An old friend," he said.